'Why not let date for you?'

Jack's hand went out to touch a wet strand of hair that had fallen over her brow, then he traced a line under her chin and down her neck with his finger, a faint smile on his lips. Frankie tensed at his touch.

'You're so kind, Frankie,' he sighed. 'But, no, I... I think I know the kind of person I need—so don't bother your friend.'

He bent towards her and brushed her forehead in a light kiss, then stepped back and smiled at her with those cobalt blue eyes. The atmosphere suddenly became intimate, quiet and still, as if something momentous was going to happen. Before she knew what she was doing, Frankie put her arm round his neck and drew his face down to hers, her lips pressing softly against his cheek... She wanted to show how much she appreciated his compassion—that was all, wasn't it?

'We must look out for each other,' she whispered.

Judy Campbell is from Cheshire. As a teenager she spent a great year at high school in Oregon, USA, as an exchange student. She has worked in a variety of jobs, including teaching young children, being a secretary and running a small family business. Her husband comes from a medical family, and one of their three grown-up children is a GP. Any spare time—when she's not writing romantic fiction—is spent playing golf, especially in the Highlands of Scotland.

Recent titles by the same author:

THE PREGNANT GP
THE REGISTRAR'S SECRET
THE DOCTOR'S SECRET BABY

THE DOCTOR'S LONGED-FOR BRIDE

BY

JUDY CAMPBELL

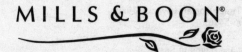

MILLS & BOON®

All the characters in this book have no existence outside the imagination of the author, and have no relation whatsoever to anyone bearing the same name or names. They are not even distantly inspired by any individual known or unknown to the author, and all the incidents are pure invention.

First published in Great Britain 2006
Harlequin Mills & Boon Limited,
Eton House, 18-24 Paradise Road, Richmond, Surrey TW9 1SR

© Judy Campbell 2006

ISBN-13: 978 0 263 84769 7
ISBN-10:   0 263 84769 1

Set in Times Roman 10½ on 13¼ pt
03-1106-54965

Printed and bound in Spain
by Litografia Rosés, S.A., Barcelona

THE DOCTOR'S LONGED-FOR BRIDE

PROLOGUE

IT WAS HOT in the park—people lay basking on the grass under the shade of the trees and children splashed in the paddling pool, their happy squeals carrying over to Francesca holding Abby by the hand.

'Can I go in there?' asked the little girl imploringly, tugging Francesca towards the pool. *'Please!'*

Francesca laughed. 'You can if Daddy says so—but you're due at a party soon and he may not want you to get wet.'

'He doesn't mind me getting wet—really!' the child assured her, then she started bouncing excitedly up and down. 'Look—he's coming now. Let's ask him, shall we?'

A tall man with thick russet-coloured hair and rimless glasses that gave him a rather studious look ran up to them. 'Sorry to keep you, Francesca—the clinic was running late as usual and I couldn't get away. Thanks a ton for minding Abby.'

'No trouble, Jack. I love looking after her, as you know.' Francesca grinned at him. 'And I'm not surprised you're late— I've never known a Saturday clinic end early.'

Abby pushed in between them and wound her arms round

her father's legs. 'Please, Daddy, let me paddle in the little pool. I won't get very wet you know…'

Both adults laughed and the man lifted Abby up in his arms and kissed her cheek. 'Difficult not to get very wet in water,' he teased. 'Go on, then—just for a minute, sweetheart. Better take off that dress, though. You'll soon dry out in this heat before we go to Sam's party.'

Francesca helped Abby take off her dress and the little girl scampered joyfully towards the pool, her russet curly hair springing up and down.

'She's such a dear little girl,' said Francesca, her eyes following Abby. 'So bright and bubbly. You must be very proud of her Jack.'

Jack sighed. 'Of course I am. I just wish Sue was here to see her, that's all. It seems so hard that she'll never watch Abby growing up.'

Francesca looked at him sympathetically. He and his late wife had made such a great couple, devoted to each other and absolutely besotted with their little daughter when she had been born. When Sue had died he had been devastated, and Francesca felt he had never recovered from her loss.

She and Jack started to stroll towards the paddling pool after Abby, and Francesca squeezed his arm.

'You must be lost without Sue,' she said gently. 'But you've done so well on your own with Abby.'

'Thanks in large part to you.' Jack smiled at her. 'I've really appreciated you helping out when I've been stuck, you know—like you did today, picking her up from the childminder and looking after her when you'd already done a long stint in A and E.'

'If I can't help look after my fiancé's niece from time to time, it's a poor lookout. It works both ways anyway. You're Damian's brother-in-law and it's been good to be able to unload some of my worries on you while he's in South America.'

'No regrets about me introducing you to someone who's away more than he's here?' asked Jack.

'Don't be silly. Love doesn't dilute with distance, you know! I'll always be grateful to you.' She sighed. 'I wish I could go out and see him, but he's adamant that I shouldn't because of the unrest in the area at the moment.'

A vivid picture of her first meeting with Damian sprang into Frankie's mind—a lovely summer's evening by the river in the garden of a country pub. Jack had persuaded her to come and have a drink after a gruelling day's work and meet his brother-in-law who had been back in England for a short time. A charismatic man with thick fair hair had been holding forth in the middle of a group of people in a witty and exuberant way about life on the island off South America where he'd worked. He'd had the confident and easy manner of someone who had not been embarrassed to be the centre of attention—very different from Jack's diffident and modest demeanour.

Frankie could recall the exact moment when Damian had turned round and seen her by Jack's side. Damian's eyes had held hers for a full minute, it seemed, then his gaze had shifted slowly up and down her body in a frank look of admiration and lust. If any other man had behaved like that, Frankie thought wryly, she'd have told them where to get off, but something about him had made her melt like snow in the desert. Damian had abandoned the group he'd been with, including a wistful-looking blonde girl, and had spent the rest of the evening with Frankie. And after that she'd fallen for him.

'Any news from him?' asked Jack.

Frankie turned a glowing face to Jack, her dark brown eyes sparkling. 'I was going to tell you—I had an e-mail this morning, saying he's coming back next week—isn't that great? It's been six months since I've seen him.'

Jack looked startled, almost shocked. 'He'll be here as soon as that?' He stared ahead for a moment, watching his daughter splashing energetically in the pool, then he said slowly, 'So I suppose you'll be fixing a date for the wedding, then?'

He watched her eager and excited expression, and she laughed. 'Oh, I expect so, as soon as possible. And, of course, you'll be best man, won't you? I know Damian would want you to be.'

A look of slight embarrassment crossed his face. 'He may have other plans. I don't want to assume that he wants me…'

'Nonsense!' declared Francesca. 'He was Susan's brother and I know that he would want to include you in the ceremony. If Susan had been alive she would have been my brides-maid—now it would be wonderful if Abby could do that for me instead. I'd love that and I'm sure she would, too. She'd look adorable in a special dress…'

Jack's expression cleared and he smiled down at her, his blue eyes twinkling. 'If you're sure you want a four-year-old hanging onto your train. It could be dangerous!' He shot a look at his watch, then called out to his daughter, 'Come on, Abby—time to go to Sam's party now. Let's put your dress back on!'

Abby ran obediently out of the pool, giggling as some

other children splashed her with water. 'I'm coming!' she yelled. 'I'm going to get you all wet in a minute!'

Jack caught his daughter in his arms and hugged her. 'You wouldn't do that to Daddy, would you?'

'Yes, I would,' she shouted. She looked up at Francesca impishly. 'Are you going to take me to the party, too?' she asked.

Francesca was about to say that she'd be happy to stroll along with them when Jack interjected quickly. 'Francesca's given up a lot of her day already, Abby. She's got a life of her own, you know, things she's got to do without us! And when she's married to Damian, we won't see her as much as we do now.'

Abby's underlip jutted out crossly. 'I want her to come,' she muttered. 'Everyone else has mummies with them as well as daddies. They'd think she was my mummy…'

A shadow crossed Jack's strong face. 'You'll have to make do with me, sweetheart,' he said gently.

'I really don't mind coming with you, Jack,' said Francesca, her heart going out in sympathy to the little girl.

Jack's eyes flicked momentarily across to Francesca, meeting hers for a fleeting moment, an unreadable expression crossing his face. Then he shook his head. 'No, no,' he said briskly. 'No need for that. I'll see you at St Mary's on Monday. Thanks again for your help today. Come on, Abby, love, I'll carry you across the park.'

He strode off with the child in his arms, and Francesca watched them go with a funny feeling of regret—she loved being with them and, she had to confess, being a mother-figure to little Abby. She'd half hoped that she and Jack could have gone and had a cup of tea while Abby was at the party— it would have been good to have had a chat, discuss the branch of the family business Damian was hoping to set up when he returned home, and also talk about Abby and her new school. She was surprised that Jack hadn't suggested it—they often spent Saturday afternoon together.

She turned and walked slowly back to the little terraced house she rented at the edge of the common, somehow feeling rather flat and deflated. Then she shook herself mentally. Jack was right—she had a life of her own, and Damian would be back soon. She wouldn't have to rely on Jack to help her when anything in the house needed doing, and equally she wouldn't be able to act as his escort when he needed someone to go to the theatre with or to a supper party with close friends. She'd got used to a certain way of life when Damian had gone to South America—and now, after six months, things would have to change!

Francesca paused at the doorstep and looked back across the park, where Jack's diminishing figure could just be seen disappearing amongst the trees. She'd got to know him well these last few months and they'd become really good friends—he was so trustworthy and such fun. She wondered whether it was too soon after Sue's death to find a girlfriend for him. Nevertheless, she would keep a lookout for a suitable girl and perhaps they could go out as a foursome. Feeling cheered by that thought, she went into the house.

CHAPTER ONE

'YOU JUST WOULDN'T *believe* what it was like last night—just completely scary. I didn't know whether to laugh or cry!'

Corey Davidson flopped down on the pub bench, and Francesca Lovatt looked up from the letter she was absorbed in reading. 'What, Corey?' she said absently, then her face cleared. 'Oh, yes…the speed-dating evening. I thought it was supposed to be fun?'

Corey groaned, her round face a picture of dejection. 'I'm just no good at thinking of questions to ask people I've nothing in common with. You know I hate all sports and every man there seemed to be heavily into football, golf or tennis…'

'Perhaps you ought to join a tennis club, then,' suggested Frankie, putting the letter back in her pocket with a sigh and feeling slightly sick from the shock of its contents.

Corey scowled. 'No fear. And it was deeply humiliating, too—I didn't get *anyone* wanting my phone number!'

'Did you want any of their phone numbers?' enquired Frankie, unable to help smiling at her friend's comically woe-begone face, despite the news she'd just received.

'No,' admitted Corey. She looked enviously at Frankie.

'You're so lucky to have Damian—did you fix a date for the wedding when he was over?'

Frankie swallowed hard. 'Not yet… You know he had to go back to South America unexpectedly when the manager of the factory died, so he was only here for a few days.' She bit her lip and looked sadly at her friend, then added slowly, 'Actually, I've just had a letter. He…he doesn't know when he can come home—and he doesn't want me to go out there because of the unrest in that area at the moment. And…well, there is something more…'

Her voice trailed off and Corey put her hand sympathetically on Frankie's arm. 'I'm so sorry, Frankie. Here am I, rabbiting on about my ghastly evening and you've got worries of your own. You must be fed up.'

Frankie pushed the letter towards Corey. 'Read the last part,' she said. 'It was quite a shock I can tell you.'

'Not before I get us both a drink,' declared her friend, jumping up from the bench. 'I have a feeling it's bad news and after the day we've had in A and E we need a pick-me-up—preferably alcoholic!'

She pushed her way through the crowded bar and Frankie leant back on her seat and closed her eyes for a second, propping her tired legs up on the table crossbar to relieve the pressure on her feet. It had been a long day in Casualty and she wasn't at all sure that coming to the crowded smoky atmosphere of the Drover's Arms had been the best idea, especially after reading Damian's letter. Perhaps the full import of it hadn't hit her yet because she felt rather numb, detached almost from what Damian had said.

Corey returned with two white wine spritzers and looked

at Frankie's pale face and the dark rings under her eyes. 'You look knackered Frankie—have a swig of this,' she declared, handing over the drink.

'I do feel shattered,' admitted Frankie. 'But you must be as well—we were run off our feet after dealing with that multiple RTA this afternoon. We're so short-staffed at the moment, especially now Larry Higson's left.'

'Yeah, it's a shame about Larry taking off. It can't be much fun for you, being the only registrar on the unit sometimes. Anyway, help is at hand—someone's coming in his place tomorrow. I met him at lunchtime.'

Frankie raised her brows. 'I'm glad to hear that, but how come I'm the last to find out? Do we know who it is—anyone local?'

Corey shrugged. 'I don't think so. Jack someone or other—wants to get a consultancy in A and E. Must be mad!'

'Jack?' A momentary flicker of interest. 'Do you know his surname?'

'No idea, but he's a bit of all right.' Corey giggled. 'Perhaps he's a better bet than speed-dating. Think you know him?'

'I shouldn't think so. I did work with someone called Jack at my last job, but he disappeared quite suddenly and there must be hundreds of registrars with that name.'

Jack Herrick, Damian's brother-in-law… Frankie sighed. She still hadn't got over the extraordinary shock when Jack had left without warning, not even staying to see Damian who had been due to come home the following week. It had been a complete mystery as to why Jack should have gone without saying a word to her, just a cursory note left pinned on her locker at work and a brief mention of hoping to see her again, probably at her wedding to Damian. Later she'd heard on the grapevine that he'd become engaged, which had surprised her as she had not known he had even wanted to go out with anyone after losing Sue.

There was no doubt that Jack's abrupt departure without explanation had hurt. He'd been a comforting link with Damian. She'd thought their mutual support system had helped them both—he'd been like a rock when Damian had had to go abroad and sort out the old family business, a shoulder to cry on, in fact. In turn, he'd talked to her about his little girl, and the difficulties involved in being a widower with a child. They'd worked together at the large casualty department at St Mary's hospital, thirty miles from the infirmary, and Frankie was sure she'd developed a close and relaxed friendship with him. After all, she was going to be a part of his family in that she was marrying his brother-in-law. It had been a slap in the face when he'd just disappeared without even the courtesy of a goodbye.

She gave a mental shrug of dismissal as Corey's voice broke into her thoughts. All that was history—she was at another hospital now and only concerned with the present and what Damian had written to her.

'Now, let me see this letter—looks as if it's upset you,' said Corey.

Frankie held it out. 'You'll see why when you read it, but I'd rather the whole department didn't know yet.'

Corey looked scornfully at her friend. 'As if,'she protested. 'You know me better than that.'

Her eyes widened as she scanned the sheet of paper, then she put down the letter and whistled softly, shaking her head and looking in disbelief at Frankie. 'Oh, God, Frankie, I don't believe this—he must be mad! He can't mean all that about not wanting to be engaged any more,' she added vehemently. 'He loved you, wanted to marry you. There must be some reason for him to break it off so suddenly.'

Frankie shrugged, and although she tried to keep her voice light, there was a bitter edge to her words. 'I thought he loved me, too. When he came over he gave me the impression that he couldn't bear to leave me…' She gave a shaky laugh. 'I must have missed something, mustn't I?'

Corey looked at her friend, full of sympathy. 'Why didn't he tell you when he was over here? Too bloody cowardly by half. He left it until he'd gone back—the rat!'

'Perhaps he was just trying to do the right thing by me,' said Francesca flatly. 'He won't be back for at least a year and maybe he doesn't want to tie me down for all that time…'

'Tie himself down more like,' said Corey cynically. 'What do you really think, Frankie?'

Frankie stared down at the letter on the table in front of her then looked up at Corey. 'I think you're right,' she admitted. 'It's him that wants to be free, although he doesn't mention that there's anyone else. Anyway, what's the point of being engaged to someone if they don't love you any more? I would like to know the truth, though—why he's suddenly dumped me…'

She felt tears pressing against her eyes and took a long drink to quell the telltale sobs that threatened to choke her. Corey was right—why hadn't he had the guts to tell her when they had been together? She felt a hollow empty feeling of rejection coupled with a gathering anger that he'd never hinted that his feelings for her might have changed. It was all so sudden, out of the blue.

'What will you do?' asked Corey, putting her arm round Frankie and hugging her comfortingly.

Frankie pulled a snapshot out of her pocket and scanned it bleakly. 'I can't kill the man,' she said in an attempt at humour, 'but I'm going to have to put him out of my mind somehow…'

Corey looked over her shoulder at the picture. 'Yeah—he's drop-dead gorgeous all right, but he must be a moron to let someone like you go.' She scanned Frankie's heart-shaped face, framed by thick chestnut hair, and grinned at her. 'It's my bet that within the year another twenty men will be after you!'

Frankie tightened her lips and tore the photo into little pieces. 'I doubt it, Corey, and I can tell you that at this moment in time the last thing I'll be searching for is a man…what's the point? You give your heart to someone—and for what? You're rejected with no reason given, no warning. It's as if you might never even have existed, the past years wiped out, forgotten about…'

Corey took Frankie's hands and squeezed them. 'Darling Frankie, don't let him get you down…you're worth so much more than he is!'

She smiled at Frankie who even managed a watery smile in return. 'Don't worry,' Frankie said staunchly. 'I hope I'm made of sterner stuff than that…'

But it was going to be tough, she reflected as she watched the other people in the pub—so many of them with partners, laughing and happy. It was hard to imagine that any of them were feeling quite as desolate as she was at that moment.

A sudden bellow of noise in the room and a certain commotion around the bar made both girls spin round. The landlord, a big burly man, was pushing his way purposefully through the jostling crowd, a warning finger held up.

His angry voice floated over towards them. 'You can stop that here and now—I won't have brawling in my pub! Put that bottle down!'

There was a sound of shouting and scuffling. Corey groaned. 'Oh, no, we have enough of this at work. What the hell's going on?'

'Who suggested we should go and have a quiet drink after work?' murmured Frankie sardonically. 'Perhaps next time we'll go to the café on the high street for a nice cup of tea…'

A chair was thrown against the bar, and a scream came from a woman in the little knot of onlookers. Then there was a general intake of breath as someone fell to the floor and two or three men began to wrestle with a tall youth in a black leather jacket and shaven head. Gradually he was manhandled to the wall and pinned against it with his arms behind his back. The figure on the floor lay still.

'I only tapped him one,' shouted the youth. 'It was just a tickle—no reason for him to go down. He was threatening me with a bottle… He's dead drunk, out for the count.'

Frankie's eyes met Corey's in humorous exasperation. 'Here we go—sounds rather familiar doesn't it?' she murmured. 'Better go and look, I suppose.'

They pushed their way through the small crowd of gawping customers, and Frankie said quietly to the landlord, who was bending down by the fallen man with two other people. 'I'm a doctor and my friend's a nurse—perhaps we'd better see how this man is if you'd just let us through…'

The landlord looked at her with relief and stepped back. 'Thank God—I'd be grateful. This is the last thing I need. No decent punters want to come to a place where brawls are happening. The police and ambulance are on their way—but Lord knows how long they'll be.' He glanced down at the supine figure before him. 'This guy looks as if he's had a skinful—completely blotto. What do you think?'

The young man had started groaning, his eyes fluttering in a grey-tinged face and his limbs moving restlessly from side to side.

'He's still with us at any rate,' said Frankie, and squatted down beside him, holding his wrist to take his pulse, touching his forehead with her hand. She looked up at the curious on-lookers. 'Anyone know this man's name?'

'Gary Hemp,' shouted someone.

'Right, Gary,' said Frankie, bending low over the man. 'Can you hear me?'

Gary muttered something unintelligible, and Frankie pulled down his lower eyelid to look at his pupils. 'No reaction,' she murmured. 'He's sweating and his heart rate's up.' She looked up at Corey, frowning. 'But something doesn't add up here. Did you see where he was hit?' she asked the landlord, who was now standing over her with folded arms and pursed lips.

'It didn't look a full-blooded punch,' he admitted, 'more a swipe that glanced against his chin, but he went down like a felled tree.'

'It's possible he's got concussion from hitting his head on the floor,' pondered Frankie, 'But it's a carpeted area here. I wouldn't have thought...' She bent forward and smelt the man's breath, then looked up at Corey with a slightly trium-phant smile. 'I think I've got it, Corey. Not sure if I'm right, though. What do you think?'

Corey knelt next to Gary and put her face close to his. 'He

smells of alcohol, that's for sure…but there is something else on his breath, too, which reminds me of nail polish. It's acetone, isn't it?'

Frankie nodded. 'My guess is he's diabetic, and he's got alcohol-induced hypoglycaemia. It probably didn't help when he was involved in a fight. At least we know what we're trying to cope with when the ambulancemen get here.'

A man from the watching crowd called out, 'That's right, Doc—he's diabetic. Has to inject himself every day.'

'Ah, yes, look at that, Corey—a pinprick on his thumb.'

Frankie turned the man's hand towards Corey, who put a cushion from one of the chairs under Gary's head and covered him with a rug the barman handed to her.

'Is he in danger?' asked the landlord looking anxiously at the figure on the floor.

'If he's not treated, he could be,' admitted Frankie.

'In what way? What can it do to him?' asked the landlord. 'I thought he'd just had a skinful.'

'A diabetic who takes alcohol can suffer an unnatural surge of insulin, and that can absorb too much of the glucose in his blood. That affects the nervous system, which in turn could lead to brain damage,' she explained.

'Bloody hell,' said the landlord. He gazed nervously at the youth and wiped his brow with a handkerchief. 'Will he be all right, then?'

The sound of a siren whining down to silence came from outside and two policemen and a paramedic appeared at the door. The two girls exchanged relieved looks and Corey murmured, 'The cavalry's arrived, thank God. Once we've got some glucose into him he'll improve.'

The paramedic strode over to the injured man and then looked at Frankie and Corey in surprise. 'I thought I'd said goodbye to you two about an hour ago—after we brought in those RTA victims. Don't you have a home to go to?' He knelt down beside Frankie. 'What's happened to this gentleman?'

'I'm pretty sure it's alcohol-induced hypolglycaemia,' said Frankie. 'I suggest you give him fifty grams of glucose intravenously, and then you can take him back to hospital and get him in balance again. His name's Gary Hemp.'

'I'll do a quick blood test with a Haemastix strip,' said the paramedic, opening his medical bag. He withdrew a little blood from the patient's arm and put a blob on the strip. 'Yup—his blood sugar's way down,' he remarked. 'Better get some glucagen into him.'

He took out a prepacked needle and phial of glucose, which he swiftly injected into the man. 'Involved in a fight, was he? He's got a cut lip…'

'It wasn't my fault,' shouted the other youth, now held by one of the policemen. 'I told you, he suddenly went beserk—tried to kill me with a broken bottle, he did! I wasn't doing anything to him at all, just talking about football,' he added in an aggrieved voice.

'He could very well have got aggressive just before he went down,' murmured Frankie to the other policeman. 'People who are out of balance with their insulin can sometimes become very hostile—change their character completely.'

Gradually the young man's eyes flickered open and he looked in a bewildered way at the faces above him.

'You're all right, Gary—just had some imbalance with your insulin,' said the paramedic. 'Forget to take it today, did you? Don't worry, son, we're just going to take you to hospital to check you out.'

The youth moaned faintly. 'What's happened?' he croaked as he was being stretchered out of the pub. The other youth's details were taken down by the policeman. Gradually the on-lookers drifted back to the bar, and the paramedic turned to Frankie and Corey as he picked up his medical bag.

'I know you're off duty,' he said pleadingly, 'but you couldn't come back with us, could you? Just heard that there's been a general call for more staff—a wall's collapsed in the high street and there's several people trapped. Some of the A and E staff have gone out to the scene.'

Corey groaned. 'I was going to have a lovely bath, watch telly all evening and eat really unhealthy food…'

She looked enquiringly at Frankie, who shrugged and nodded. 'Go on, then, tell them we'll be there in a minute.' After all, she thought bleakly, she wasn't going to be doing anything else when she went home—not even making plans for a wedding any more.

Denniston Vale Infirmary was a sprawling Victorian Hospital with modern additional wings tacked onto it in random fashion, their pockmarked walls contrasting oddly with the magnificent stonework of the original building. It stood on a hill at the edge of Denniston town, an imposing clock tower rising from the centre of the building and impressive stone steps leading up to the front entrance, although the ambulances went round the back where the casualty department was situated.

As Frankie's car swung round the corner to the staff car park, they could see three ambulances lined up, with patients being lifted out on trolleys then being pushed through to the unit. Two police cars were parked to the side of the ambulances, their blue lights still flashing, and a harassed-looking plump nurse with a clipboard was watching the proceedings.

'Looks a biggy,' groaned Corey. 'My feet are killing me already at the thought of it.'

'Come on,' said Frankie. 'You won't notice your feet once you get going.'

'Don't you believe it,' retorted Corey. 'And look who's on duty—fusspot Sister Kenney. That's going to make my day.'

She jumped out of the car and they began to trot towards the entrance.

'What did I tell you?' she murmured, as the nurse stepped towards them and wrote something on the clipboard. 'Evening, Sister Kenney.'

The woman nodded to her, a brief smile replacing her worried frown for a minute. 'Thank you for coming in— I'm really grateful.' She waved vaguely towards the bustle of ambulances and stretchers. 'As you can see, we're very much stretched at the moment. We've got Mr Burton from Orthopaedics helping to deal with the injuries from the collapsed wall and I've managed to persuade the senior nursing officer to loan us some nurses from Medical.'

'That must have taken some doing,' murmured Frankie.

Sister Kenney allowed herself a small triumphant grin. 'It's about time they helped us out. Now, please, would you look at a woman with chest pains in the end cubicle? She's a Mrs Jepson, just come in while all this brouhaha was going on, and all three theatres and the emergency room are in use. She needs her vital signs monitored—I'll leave you to do that, Dr Lovatt.'

It took just a few minutes to scramble into their hospital greens and make their way to the large central area surrounded by cubicles. A large woman lying propped up on a bed in the end cubicle looked at Frankie and Corey with frightened eyes. She had the familiar expression of many patients who found themselves in a totally alien situation with people they didn't know, surrounded by sights and sounds they probably associated more with television dramas than their own life. She was clutching the hand of a small man sitting by her side.

'Am I having a heart attack?' she asked tremulously. 'I've got these awful pains, and my husband thinks it could be a myocardial….' She looked helplessly at the small man.

'Myocardial infarction,' he said rather smugly.

The woman's voice had started to rise on the edge of panic, her mouth trembling, and Frankie put a reassuring hand on her arm, trying to calm her patient and reduce her stress levels. As usual, she found herself using well-worn platitudes, which nevertheless were soothing in their familiarity, comforting phrases that the woman would have known all her life.

'It's Mrs Jepson, isn't it?' she said kindly. 'Now, please, don't worry—I want you to try and relax. We're going to run a series of tests that will help to tell us what's causing these pains. It could be a variety of things and we mustn't jump to conclusions. But you're in the right place to find these things out.'

The small man nodded sagely. 'That's what I told her, Doctor. I said it could also be indigestion—she had chips and sausages just an hour ago, and an apple pie, didn't you, love?'

'So you are Mr Jepson?' asked Corey, attaching a monitor to the woman's arm that ran a trace of the patient's blood oxygen sats and blood pressure on a screen.

'I am indeed,' said the man. 'We were going to the cinema—just paid for the tickets as a matter of fact when she was took bad.'

'This came on quite suddenly, then?' asked Frankie, watching the screen monitor.

The woman shifted restlessly. 'Well, I've not been feeling quite myself for a few days—had this horrible pain near my heart.' She indicated an area in the centre of her chest. 'But it's got worse and worse this evening.'

Mr Jepson looked at her indignantly. 'You never said, Norma. I didn't know you'd been feeling off…'

'Didn't want to worry you,' his wife said, rather sullenly.

'Well, your blood pressure's OK,' said Frankie. 'Have you had an operation lately, or an injury that's kept you in bed?'

Mrs Jepson shook her head, and her husband leaned forward eagerly. 'You thinking of a blood clot on the lungs, Doctor? Could it be that?'

His wife gave a start of horror and Frankie's eyes met Corey's in a brief exasperated glance. Mr Jepson seemed intent on alarming his wife as much as possible, and making a nervous patient even more apprehensive. If he wanted to send his wife's blood pressure sky high, he was going the best way about it, thought Frankie, hiding her irritation by smiling winningly at him.

'We'll be some time examining your wife, so why don't you go and have a coffee from the machine in the waiting room while you can? When you come back, we may have more news to tell you.'

The man looked hesitant. 'Surely it's better that I stay and keep Norma calm?'

'It'll be best to sit with your wife when we've finished our assessment. These cubicles are small and it gets a little crowded in here, as you can see…'

The man stumped off unwillingly, only turning back at the door to comment to his wife, 'If it's a heart attack, you'll be in here for days, you know.'

Norma looked mournfully at Frankie. 'We were going on holiday next week—looks like we'll have to cancel it if I'm going to be here for ages.'

'You may be feeling much better soon,' said Corey brightly. 'Wait until we've had the results of your blood tests…'

'And we'll run a cardiac trace to check your heart,' added Frankie.

The phone rang at the main nurses' station and Corey left to answer it. Frankie leant forward to listen to the woman's chest through her stethoscope. When she put the stethoscope on the area of skin below her breasts, Mrs Jepson flinched.

'Don't touch me there—it's absolute agony, that!' she gasped.

Frankie looked more closely at the area she'd just touched and frowned. 'Did you know you've got a rash here…quite a distinctive rash?'

'There wasn't anything there yesterday.'

Frankie pulled the overhead light so that it focussed on the red weal across the woman's chest. 'You know, Mrs Jepson,' she said slowly, 'I think that this could be a clue to the mystery of your pain.'

Mrs Jepson gave a sharp intake of breath. 'It's my heart, isn't it?' she said in a quiet voice, as if bracing herself for very bad news. 'Have you heard something odd through that instrument?'

'Your heart and chest sounded fine—it's what I can see that's quite illuminating. You've got a band of blistery little spots across your chest, which have probably just come out. Does it feel itchy?'

'A little. It's painful when you touch that area, and there's a horrible pain deep into the chest....'

The door opened behind Frankie and a deep voice said, 'Was someone wanting a heart trace in here?'

Frankie glanced towards the tall figure who'd entered the cubicle, then her mouth dropped as she did a double-take at the tall man with rimless glasses and russet hair who stood in front of her. Was she imagining things or was it really the familiar figure of Jack Herrick?

'My God…Jack!' she exclaimed. 'What on earth are you doing here?'

Jack stared back at Frankie, also stunned. 'I might ask you the same thing,' he said. 'I didn't know you were working at the infirmary…'

'I have been for six months…You must be the new registrar that Corey told me about.'

Mrs Jepson looked from one doctor to the other, interest making her forget her discomfort for the moment.

'You two old friends, then?' she asked.

Jack smiled apologetically. 'I'm sorry, Mrs Jepson. As you can see, we're both a bit surprised to see each other. And yes, we go back quite a long way. Now, first things first—I believe you've been having chest pains…'

'I'd like you to take a look at this rash, Dr Herrick,' said Frankie, her mind still buzzing with the surprise of seeing him. 'I'd be interested to know what you think.'

He inspected the reddened area closely for a moment, then looked across at Frankie. 'Not much doubt about it—a good example of Herpes zoster, I would say.'

'What's that?' asked Mrs Jepson.

'I suppose you had chickenpox when you were a child?'

She looked puzzled. 'Yes. All my brothers and sisters had it at the same time—Mum nearly went mad!'

'Then your past has come back to haunt you, I think. The virus has been reactivated, and all the signs point to it being shingles…'

'Shingles?' repeated Mrs Jepson, gazing at both doctors in astonishment.

'That's right,' said Frankie. 'The pain in your body is caused by the shingles. In fact, the virus is affecting the nerve endings—that's why it's so sore. The rash often doesn't appear for a few days.'

The woman lay back on the pillows. 'I can't believe it,' she said. 'Is that all it is?'

Frankie smiled. 'It's not very nice, I'm afraid, but it's better than having a heart attack! Mind you, I still think we need to run these tests on you. We don't want to assume that just because you've got shingles there aren't any other problems.'

'That's one thing my Bert never thought of!' Mrs Jepson looked rather triumphantly at Frankie and Jack, clearly pleased to have put one over on her husband. 'I wonder what's brought on shingles, then? I've not been near anyone with chickenpox…'

'It doesn't work that way. Often it's because you've been under stress for some reason and perhaps your immune system's been compromised—or possibly because you've been on steroid treatment.'

'That makes sense,' said Mrs Jepson gloomily. 'I've had that much trouble with our son—he's been in trouble with the police, taking drugs, joy-riding cars and I don't know what else. I've been out of my mind with worry.'

Jack nodded sympathetically. 'That sort of thing could trigger an attack. We could try you on an antiviral drug which might reduce the severity of the active stage and minimise nerve damage.'

Frankie broke open a sterile needle pack and nodded, adding, 'In the meantime, we'll make sure that this is the only problem you have. Dr Herrick will run a trace on your heart when I've taken some blood for tests.'

She wound a cuff round the patient's arm to make it easier to find a vein. Jack watched as she completed the task and she felt his gaze on her. She wondered if he felt any embarrassment at all, bumping into her like this. Was he going to explain why he'd just vanished into thin air and had he any idea how much he'd hurt her? Not, she conceded wryly, as much as his precious brother-in-law had hurt her—but it had been damned rude to vanish without explanation. Recently men seemed to have treated her pretty badly, she reflected grimly.

Her patient's plaintive voice brought Frankie guiltily back to the matter in hand. 'I hope I don't faint, Doctor—I have a horror of needles. Have you nearly finished yet? I can't bear to look at what you're doing.'

Frankie drew some blood into the needle and smiled reassuringly at Mrs Jepson. 'There we go! All done now. We'll soon get the tests back.'

Mrs Jepson lay back on the pillows and looked up at them

both. 'Thank goodness that's over! And fancy me having shingles! I can't wait to tell Bert.'

Frankie moved over to the shelf to pick up the phials for the blood. She brushed past Jack and flicked him a caustic glance. 'I was led to believe you'd moved miles away from here when you left,' she said in a low voice.

Was there slight embarrassment in his eyes when they met hers? 'That's true. I went down to London, but things didn't work out quite how I hoped. However, it looks like we'll be working together again—it'll seem like old times,' he commented smilingly.

Not quite like old times, thought Frankie. She'd thought that Jack and she had had a free and easy relationship before— now she couldn't help feeling resentful at working again with a colleague who had brushed off their friendship so casually. Now another dynamic had entered the picture: she was no longer engaged to Damian. She and Jack did not have that connection any more, and perhaps it was better that way— she did not want to be reminded of Damian, who had finished with her as casually as he would a boring book, with no explanation. That part of her life was over and, as far as she was concerned working with Jack Herrick again was going to be just another job.

CHAPTER TWO

THE NEXT HOUR was manic, the pressure on Casualty building up with the usual emergency cases as well as those involved in the collapsed wall. It was ten o'clock before the situation eased and Frankie and Corey met in the staffroom.

'That's three fractures, an overdose, a scalding and a drunk who nearly suffocated on his own vomit, topped off with Sister Kenney telling me to help that dozy porter, Tim, move six oxygen cylinders from the passage. I've had enough!' Corey flopped dramatically back on the sofa. 'Next time we're asked to do overtime, they can get someone else!'

Frankie smiled. 'Go on—you know you love it really. Now, get that coffee down you.'

She handed Corey a mug. Corey took a sip and sighed. 'Even this instant sludge tastes good at the moment. By the way, have you bumped into knockout Jack Herrick yet, our new registrar? I could hardly concentrate on what I was doing…'

'It turns out that he was the man I used to work with at St Mary's,' said Frankie. 'It was a surprise, seeing him again.' She looked ruefully at Corey. 'He also happens to be Damian's brother-in-law.'

'Ouch! How bizarre is that!' said Corey in surprise. 'So does he know what that rat has done to you?'

'I haven't got round to it yet. I suppose I'll have to tell him later. It was through Jack that I met Damian originally.'

'Well, I hope Jack will be suitably horrified.' Corey looked speculatively at Frankie. 'I guess you'll know a bit about this gorgeous Jack, won't you? I suppose he's married with about four kids.'

'He's a widower with one little girl. His wife, Damian's sister, was killed in a car accident two years ago, but—'

'I knew there'd be a "but,"' said Corey with a grimace.

'I did hear he was engaged and I don't know why he's come back to this area.'

'Just my luck. Ah, well, my own lovely warm bed beckons.' Corey hauled herself out of the sofa. 'See you Monday, Frankie. Sleep well.'

She went out as Sister Kenney bustled in, her blue uniform straining over her plump bosom and the usual harassed expression on her face. 'Is there any coffee in that pot? I must have something before I start filing my admissions register in the office. I hope we're on top of things now.'

Frankie looked at her sympathetically. People tended to make fun of Sister Kenney and her fussy manner, but she was a well-organised woman who tried to do her best for the staff and the patients. Frankie handed her a mug.

'Do you need me any more?' she asked.

'No. You get off now—and thanks for coming in. Even with our new registrar, we couldn't have coped without you. Have you met him, by the way? He's called Jack Herrick and I must say I'm favourably impressed so far.'

'I used to work with him at my last job. And yes, he'll be good to have on the team.'

Sister raised her eyebrows. 'Really? That's excellent news. You'll know each other's methods, then.'

As if on cue, the door was pushed open and Jack walked in. Sister Kenney gave him a wide smile.

'I believe you know each other already...I didn't realise that you and Frankie used to be colleagues.' She shot a look at her watch. 'I'm sure she can fill you in on any queries you have—but I'll have to get on now and tell the nurses we borrowed from Medical that they can finish now.'

She marched out and left Frankie and Jack alone. Jack lifted the coffee-pot.

'Want a cup?' he asked.

'No, thanks, I'm going home now and I don't want any caffeine to keep me awake.'

He looked at her levelly, then said slowly, 'It's good to see you Frankie—a lovely surprise.'

Frankie nodded without smiling. She wasn't going to go overboard at seeing him again just yet. Jack was another man who hadn't behaved all that well towards her, albeit in a much milder way than Damian had.

'Yes, I thought I'd never see you again when you vanished into thin air,' she said pointedly. 'You left before I could ask you anything. I...I wondered what had happened to make you leave so abruptly.'

He grimaced. 'I'm sorry about that, Frankie. I should have spoken to you before I left and I know I owe you an explanation.'

'You don't have to tell me why you went,' said Frankie

frostily. 'It was just a little impersonal, leaving a note pinned to my locker to tell me you were leaving. I…I thought we were good friends. I think I deserved more than that.' She paused and looked at him with a raised eyebrow. 'On the other hand, was it something I did? Perhaps I upset you in some way.'

He winced slightly, then he said vehemently, 'Of course it wasn't your fault. For heaven's sake, you were my…well, my best friend. I feel ashamed that I hurt you, but…' He paused for a moment, as if thinking of how to phrase his next sentence. 'Well, the thing is, something happened—something that made me realise I had to leave immediately. Believe me, the last thing I wanted to do in the world was offend you, of all people—someone who's going to be related to me as well.'

Frankie bit her lip, that cold feeling of rejection sweeping over her again. She could see a short-term future of repeating the same information over and over again to those who'd known she'd been engaged to Damian, but there was no point in beating about the bush. The truth had to come out some time, so why not now?

'Actually, there's something you might as well know…'

He looked at her enquiringly, one eyebrow raised.

'Damian and I aren't engaged any more, Jack.' She said it baldly, almost defiantly, not willing to show how devastated she felt.

An astounded expression crossed his face, and he put his mug of coffee down on the worktop so forcefully that the liquid slopped over the rim. 'What? You…you've broken up? When did this happen? I thought you were going to organise the wedding with him when he came over just before I left for London.'

Frankie's voice hardened. 'As a matter of fact, I received the letter earlier today, if you must know. He doesn't want to get married now. And don't ask me why—I've no idea.'

'It's unbelievable,' Jack said slowly. 'You and he…well, you seemed like the perfect couple, so well matched. I thought you two would go on for ever…'

'So did I, Jack, so did I.' Frankie couldn't help the sadness reflected in her expression, but after a short silence she said brusquely, 'But it's over now—no possibility of getting back together. He's let me down. I could never trust him again, whatever the reason is that he wanted to be free of me.'

It was odd how numb she felt, as if the full shock of her broken engagement had yet to hit her properly. She looked at Jack challengingly. 'Would you have said he was untrustworthy? You've known him for many years.'

Jack shook his head in bewilderment. 'He's incredibly fearless—got me out of several sticky situations. In fact, he saved my life once when we were white-water rafting—at great risk to his own life. From that point of view I guess I found him very reliable. But this… I can't understand it. He told me he was mad about you.'

Jack stared at her, his eyes holding hers, something unreadable in their bright blue depths behind the studious-looking glasses. Frankie looked at his tall figure leaning against the cupboard, his arms crossed over his chest and the hospital greens he was wearing open at the neck. Quite suddenly she realised for the first time just how damned attractive Jack was. It was utterly ridiculous, especially in the circumstances of having just been dumped by someone she'd thought was the love of her life. Of course, she'd always considered Jack a good-looking man, but quiet and unassuming. Damian was the type of man who held the floor, enjoyed being the life and soul of the party—Jack always seemed to be an amused onlooker. Her assessment of Jack had been sisterly, regarding him as an easygoing and sympathetic companion.

Now she realised that Jack's diffident manner seemed to emphasise his appeal, and she suddenly understood that many girls would find him extremely sexy. She remembered Corey had found him drop-dead gorgeous…

With an effort she turned away sharply, giving the worktop another good polish to allow herself time to recover. How shallow could you get? She'd just been dumped by his brother-in-law, hadn't she? She wasn't supposed to have weak-at-the-knee feelings for other men!

'Let's change the subject,' she said lightly. 'I heard somewhere that you'd got engaged recently. When's the happy day?'

He smiled ruefully. 'I'm afraid that bit the dust as well. My fault—I got engaged for the wrong reasons far too quickly and it was never going to work out.'

She turned to him, genuine sympathy on her face. 'Oh, dear, you felt it was too soon after Sue's death?'

He looked down at the floor for a moment, his fists clenching together at his sides. 'That could be the reason,' he murmured.

'Better to find out now than later,' comforted Frankie.

Jack nodded, watching her as she folded the dishcloth and hung it over the taps. 'Absolutely. Getting entangled in the wrong relationship is madness—it can ruin your life. One should be totally sure you've got the right person.'

Frankie picked up her bag and her mouth twisted sadly.

'You don't have to tell me that, Jack. Perhaps Damian's done me a favour after all.' She flicked her hair back from her forehead. 'Now, tell me about Abby. I suppose she's at a local school? I have missed her, you know.'

He smiled and pulled out a photograph from his trouser pocket. 'This is her in her new school uniform—she's very proud of it.'

Frankie gazed at the photograph he passed her, and said wistfully, 'She's grown since I saw her last—inevitable, I suppose. But she looks so sweet and still very young—and very like Sue!'

Jack nodded. 'Yes, I'm relieved to say she's taken after her mother in looks. In fact Abby's the reason I've come to Denniston. My parents live here and they want to help me as much as possible with Abby, which will be great. It's not much fun, coping on your own.'

'Lovely for them, too, I imagine, to watch their little grand-daughter grow up. I'd love to see her again.'

He took off his glass and polished them, then said rather diffidently, 'Perhaps this is a bit of a cheek, but if you're in-terested and have the time, Abby's got a sports day at school next weekend—I don't suppose you'd come if you're not at work? She'd really love you to be there, I know.'

Frankie felt a little leap of pleasure—seeing Abby again would be lovely. Then she hesitated slightly, reluctant to restart a friendship that had seemed to founder so abruptly previously.

She replied lightly, 'If I'm free, I'd love to come. I'll let you know nearer the time.'

If he noticed her reserved tone, he didn't show it. 'Sure,' he said easily. 'I'll remind you about it.'

Frankie opened the door and looked back at him. 'I'll see you next week, then. Now I'm off to have a good sleep—so much has happened today I feel absolutely pole-axed!'

'I bet you do, Frankie. And I'm so sorry that this has happened.'

'Don't be. I'm not going to let it ruin my future—but I would like to know just why the hell Damian suddenly felt he couldn't love me any more!'

Her eyes bright with unshed tears, Frankie walked quickly out of the room.

Jack watched Frankie disappear and shook his head in disbelief at what she'd told him. How could Damian have finished with a girl like her—talented, fun, a knockout to look at, but most of all a kindly and generous person? The man was a fool—a restless soul who ran through money, lived life to the full and easily became bored. But even so, he'd thought that when Damian had met Frankie, his friend had found a soulmate.

Jack finished the dregs of his coffee and slumped moodily down in a chair, staring unseeingly at a poster on the wall in front of him that exhorted him to wash his hands. He remembered how thrilled his darling wife Sue had been when her brother had become engaged to Frankie. The two girls had become great friends and extremely close, seeing each other frequently—and, of course, that had helped to forge the friendship he and Frankie had had after Sue's death.

His thoughts drifted to his friendship with Frankie now and he sighed ruefully. He'd obviously hurt Frankie very much by leaving the last job so abruptly, and it was going to take time to heal the wounds of bruised friendship. Who could blame

Frankie for feeling offended when he'd gone without a word of explanation?

Jack picked up a pencil from the worktop and rolled it absently between his fingers. He'd thought he'd acted for the best when he'd left St Mary's, that he'd had no choice, but he'd handled things clumsily and had ended up jeopardising that friendship. However, after all he'd done to distance himself from her, it seemed that fate had thrown them together again, and he was back to square one—except that now Frankie was a free agent. Would that make life easier between them? He sighed and flung the pencil back on the worktop as he strode out of the room.

It was Friday afternoon and Jack was scrubbing up in the little anteroom off the small clean theatre in A and E. His patient lay with eyes closed in a face so battered it was hard to tell what sex it was. The cheeks and eyes were swollen, as were the lips, bloodied and twice normal size. Her head had been raised so that there would be the least tension possible on her face.

'Thanks for helping me out, Frankie,' said Jack.

'No worries. We're reasonably quiet now,' Frankie replied.

She started to scrub up beside him, lathering the soap well up to her elbows, massaging it between her fingers, trying to ignore the fact that she and Jack were so close together. Uneasily she had to admit that she had begun to think of Jack in a different way since that brief episode in the staff kitchen. Up until now Damian had been the only man who'd attracted her, but now she realised, that far from being a man she'd thought of more as a brother than anything else, Jack was extremely sexy in a quiet and re-strained way. She gazed at her troubled face in the mirror above the basin. Her instinct was to keep out of Jack's way as much as she could, but in a busy A and E department that was impossible.

She pulled a paper towel out of the slot and started to dry her hands briskly. She couldn't understand the sudden attraction she felt for Jack—was it a case of off with the old and on with the new? She threw the paper towel in the bin and told herself that it was a reaction to Damian breaking off the en-gagement. The last thing she wanted now was to start looking for another man in her life.

'Mr Caulfield, the plastic surgeon, is tied up with a compli-cated operation and we need to close up these wounds on Mrs Casson's face and arm as soon as possible before a risk of in-fection sets in,' Jack continued, looking at her over his mask.

Frankie nodded, hoping those piercing blue eyes couldn't see her thoughts inside her head. 'Poor woman. We don't want to have to open them up later and risk scarring. What on earth happened to her?'

'Some charming youths relieved her of her purse while she was shopping,' he replied grimly. 'I only wish I could use my scalpel on them in a place they won't forget.'

They made their way over to the patient. Mrs Casson's eyes were opened now, fearful and apprehensive. 'What are you going to do?' she whispered.

'We're going to take care of you, Mrs Casson,' said Jack in his calm, firm voice. 'You're in safe hands. We'll do a bit of stitching and clean up these wounds. It'll take some time for the swelling to go down, but in a few days you'll be back to normal.' He grinned down at her and patted her shoulder. 'Don't worry, we're brilliant at embroidery.'

The woman attempted a stiff little smile at Jack's reassuring manner and joke, visibly relaxing, and Jack was able to assess to a small degree the range of movement Mrs Casson had in her face.

Corey had been checking the instruments in the tray. She swung the overhead light so that the beam was fixed on the patient's face and said, 'Mrs Casson's had an injection of Valium, just to keep her relaxed, and an anti-tetanus jab.'

'Good—then we'll make a start.'

The woman turned slightly towards Jack and said thickly, 'Will this hurt?'

Jack smiled at her kindly. 'Don't worry, Mrs Casson. I know it probably feels pretty awful at the moment, but we're going to give you some local anaesthetic and we'll stitch these deep cuts on your face—you won't feel anything—then you'll go for a scan to make sure you've no internal head injuries.'

Mrs Casson muttered something that sounded like, 'They were horrible!'

'I couldn't agree more. Did you manage to get a description of the yobs that did this to you?'

'They were all wearing hoods,' Mrs Casson mumbled. 'They reeked of drink.' A tear rolled out of her swollen eye and coursed down her cheek. 'I had all the money from the old folk for their shopping…I didn't expect anyone to do this in a supermarket….'

Her voice trailed away, and Frankie's and Jack's eyes met over their masks in sympathy. 'If it's any comfort, I believe that the police are holding three youths,' said Jack. 'But first things first—we're going to do our best to make you look as beautiful as you did before.'

'If you can make me look better than I did before, that would be good,' she whispered.

Corey held Mrs Casson's hand as the doctors began to work on the woman's face. It was a kindly gesture that always made the patient feel less isolated: it was important for her to feel the comforting contact with one of the nursing staff.

Frankie swabbed the wounds with a saline solution and Jack carefully inserted a fine-bore needle in the woman's lower cheek to numb the area to be repaired then both doctors bent over the cuts they were going to suture. Jack concentrated on the long gash in Mrs Casson's cheek, while Frankie worked on a deep cut in the woman's arm. The Valium was doing its job—the patient lay calmly, sad eyes watching them, her muscles relaxed, making it easier to work on the wounds. They used fine-filament gut which Corey passed them in threaded needles.

The gash in the arm only took a few minutes to close, but the cheek wound took longer. It was a delicate job to close the muscle and ensure that there was no pulling which could cause facial distortion. Jack worked quickly, but it was still a lengthy and finicky business. His face frowned in concentration as he matched the opposite sides of the wound to each other, careful to stitch it without stretching the skin.

Frankie and Corey watched silently, both admiring the deftness Jack showed in such a precise exercise. It was weird, working with Jack once more, reflected Frankie, looking at the way his hair was cut rather raggedly on the nape of his neck. She'd never thought she'd see him again after his abrupt disappearance, but now they seemed to have slotted back into much the same routine they'd had before except for one thing—now she was aware of him as a man with an intriguing aura of sexual attraction. It frightened her, and because she was frightened she couldn't stop thinking about it, playing with the idea of being attracted to him, as one touched a spot on one's face to see if it had disappeared.

'That's that. All done, Mrs Casson,' he said, standing up and stretching to unstiffen his back. 'You'll just go to the recovery room until they come to take you for a scan. In a few days that swelling should go down, and hopefully you'll begin to feel a lot better.'

'Thank you,' whispered Mrs Casson.

'She may feel physically better in a few days,' remarked Frankie as Mrs Casson was taken away by Tim Mackenzie, one of the porters, to the recovery room. 'But it'll be a long time before she recovers mentally from a horrible experience like that.'

Jack flung his latex gloves into a bin. 'I'd like the idiots who did it to see what they've done to her,' he said grimly. He flicked a look at his watch. 'I could do with a cup of strong tea,' he remarked. 'How about you?'

'Sounds a good idea. I'll be there in a minute when I've written up Mrs Casson's notes.'

Frankie scribbled in the drugs dosages they'd given Mrs Casson and the procedures she'd undergone, slipping the paper into the patient's folder and putting it in the tray to be filed away later. It was quiet in the unit at the moment. She could hear Sister Kenney in the office instructing Cindy Wallace, the junior nurse, on how to administer injections, and at the end of the corridor a cleaner was polishing the floor. Suddenly Frankie wasn't sure about being in the kitchen alone with Jack—then she felt a surge of annoyance with herself. Surely it hadn't come to this, that a few days after meeting the man again she was so frightened of her feelings towards him that she couldn't have a cup of tea with him? Purposefully, she turned towards the kitchen and went in.

He looked up, smiling. 'Ah, I wondered what had kept you. A cup of tea there for you—strong enough to stand the spoon in. I reckon we deserve it after dealing with poor Mrs Casson.'

Frankie sank into a chair. 'Makes you wonder what some of these people are on, that they'd do that to a woman trying to do her bit for others.' She took a sip of the tea and wrinkled her nose. 'Ouch. You're right, this is strong. Any more milk in that jug?'

He grinned and passed her the jug, and for a second their hands brushed against each other. With a jolt Frankie knew that she wasn't imagining that zinging attraction she felt when she was near Jack. Her hands shook slightly as she put the cup to her lips again. He smiled at her, his intense eyes holding hers.

'You did say that you might come to Abby's sports day tomorrow. I hope you can manage it. She really really is looking forward to seeing you. My parents will be there as well—they'd love to meet you.'

'Oh, I don't know, Jack,' Frankie replied, flustered. 'I don't want to butt in on a family occasion. Some other time perhaps….'

His face fell. 'Abby will be disappointed—and so would I. I'd really like to try and make amends for my rudeness when I left so abruptly before. Besides, aren't you practically family anyway?'

'That's not going to happen, Jack,' Frankie said firmly. 'As I told you before, I'm not going to be your sister-in-law I'm afraid.'

'I'm sorry—that was tactless of me. Still, I'm sure Abby thinks of you as an auntie.'

His expression was wistful and Frankie sighed. Perhaps she was being silly, not taking the proffered olive branch. In any case, she'd love to see Abby again, and if his parents were there, it would sort of dilute the gathering. She smiled and nodded her head.

'If you're sure—then I look forward it.'

'That's wonderful. I'll pick you up at about two o'clock.'

'No need. I'll meet you at the school field—I know where it is.'

The wall phone jangled and Frankie got up to answer it, her eyes following Jack as he left the room. She attributed the little leap of excitement she felt at the thought of the next day to seeing Abby again and nothing to do with the fact that Jack would be there.

CHAPTER THREE

FROM THE CAR park Frankie looked across the school playing fields to the knot of people waiting to see their children take part in the sports day. She hadn't felt like coming that afternoon—the post had brought several brochures about wedding venues that she'd sent off for several weeks ago and now, of course, they wouldn't be needed. That peculiar lost feeling of rejection kept coming over her in waves.

She stumped crossly over the field, glancing up at a threatening-looking sky with dark clouds massing up over the town. Her heart melted, however, when she saw Abby, standing in a line with several other children, all looking slightly overawed by the occasion of sports day. Abby was a little taller but otherwise she hadn't changed much, her curly hair framing a sweet little face. It was lovely to see Abby again and, after all, she hadn't planned anything else for the afternoon.

Frankie glanced across at Jack, his tall figure making him easy to recognize. It would be good to feel, well, almost part of a family, cheering Abby on and showing an interest in her. Bringing up a little girl by himself must be hard—no one to share in the pleasure and delight of his child when she achieved little milestones, or to worry with him when she was ill. Abby wasn't surprised that Jack had moved to be nearer his parents.

Frankie watched Abby's anxious little face as she scanned the onlookers, making sure that her father was there. Somehow she looked very vulnerable, slightly lost. She wondered if the child would remember her after so many months without seeing her, but suddenly Abby spotted Frankie walking at them and a big smile lit her face. She waved her hand towards Frankie and turned to the child next to her, pointing over to the watching adults. Her clear little voice wafted over to Frankie above the murmur of noise around her.

'That's Frankie!'

'Who's Frankie?' the little friend asked.

Frankie saw Abby flick a glance towards her again and then explained earnestly, 'She's a person that used to help look after me—she's like a mummy.'

The other child nodded. 'I see. She's instead of a Mummy, is she?'

Frankie forgot her morning's frustration in her pleasure that Abby should remember her so well after so many months, although she couldn't help being slightly embarrassed that Abby should think of her as a mother-figure! She glanced at Jack to see if he had heard, but he was talking to his parents and seemed unaware of his daughter's comments. He looked up as Frankie approached, and his face lit up, changing his reserved look and making him look younger and less austere.

'Glad you managed to come, Frankie. Abby will be delighted. Can I introduce you to my mother and father—Brian and Sheila Herrick?'

Frankie shook hands with them. 'I can see where your son and granddaughter get their colouring from, Mrs Herrick.' She smiled.

Sheila Herrick laughed. 'My hair's got more white than russet now, but it is nice to see that my original colour's been handed down. And, please, call me Sheila.'

Jack was helping to put up some folding chairs for the on-lookers and as they sat down his mother patted the chair next to her. 'Do sit down, Frankie. I feel I know you quite well already because I used to hear so much about you from Abby when you worked with Jack at St Mary's.'

'Yes. I loved looking after her occasionally when Jack was busy. I missed her so much when they left the area.'

'It was such a pity Jack had to leave so suddenly. Lovely for us that he came here, although I know he loved working at St Mary's.'

Frankie longed to ask her why she thought Jack had left, but decided to leave it and not appear too inquisitive. Mrs Herrick probably thought, as a close friend of Jack, that she would know the reason.

'And you're engaged to Damian?' continued Mrs Herrick. She chuckled. 'He was a real scallywag at school, but he and Jack became good friends in their time there. And, of course, Jack met Sue through Damian.' Mrs Herrick looked sadly at Frankie. 'She was a wonderful girl, and I know you became very friendly with her when you became engaged. Sue used to say she couldn't wait for you and Damian to get married!'

Jack's eyes met Frankie's with a rueful expression. 'Sorry, Frankie,' he murmured. 'I'm afraid I didn't get round to telling my mother about you and Damian.'

Sheila looked enquiringly at both of them. 'Have I said something out of turn?'

'Not really,' sighed Frankie. 'The fact is that Damian and I have split up—to be honest, Damian decided he didn't want to be engaged any more.'

'Oh, goodness, I have put my foot in it, haven't I?' Sheila put her hand on Frankie's arm and squeezed it, saying in a firm voice, 'Never mind, my dear. The man must be an idiot if he doesn't want a future with someone like you—and you don't want to be married to an idiot, do you? I think it may very well work out for the best…'

It was quite refreshing to hear someone with a positive twist to her broken romance. Frankie smiled back at her. 'You may be right, Sheila. Anyway, that's the attitude I'm darned well going to take. Perhaps it's been a wake-up call for me. I'm going to start putting all my energy into my career for a change.'

Sheila nodded approvingly. 'Quite right! But remember, all work and no play, Frankie… You need a bit of fun along the way!'

'That's what I intend to do,' said Frankie rather grimly. 'When I look back on the last year, I realise I've played the waiting game at home for far too long, but I feel I've put work on hold as well. Now's my chance to go for something more ambitious.'

The sound of a shrill whistle on the field made them all turn round and watch as several children scampered in front of them in a short relay race. Abby was at the forefront, her hair bobbing around her head as she threw herself into the race with determination, her little face set with concentration. She passed on the teddy bear, which was used as a baton, successfully and then joined in the shouting as the next set of children gave their all to the finishing line. She came running up to them, bursting with pride, when the race was over.

'Did you see our team win?' she demanded. 'The others dropped their teddies,' she added scornfully.

Sheila hugged the little girl to her and Abby cuddled up to her grandmother for a minute. 'Am I coming to the farm soon?' she demanded. 'I want to see the calves and those new little chicks.'

'Of course you are, my pet…the sooner the better. Look, darling, I think they want you back on the starting line now— you'd better get back.' Sheila watched her granddaughter scamper back to the rest of the children and turned back to Frankie. 'Grandchildren are so wonderful—have your parents got any?' she asked.

'I'm an only child,' said Frankie. 'And I'm not likely to have any children now for some time.' She felt a pang of guilt. 'I haven't actually told them about Damian and I yet…that's something I must do. They were so looking forward to the wedding, too.'

'It'll be a shock for them, but you ought to tell them before they find out from someone else. Your father's connected to the university, isn't he? I'm always seeing his photo in the paper!'

'It's a bit of a high-profile job,' admitted Frankie. 'Much to my mother's disgust!'

'And do they live near here?' enquired Sheila politely.

'Only about twenty miles away—a place called Market Downey. They love the village but my mother is longing to move to a smaller place instead of the huge house they have at the moment—they rattle around in it.'

'I know how she feels,' sighed Sheila. 'We'd like to give up the farm and buy a cottage soon. What we want to do is give the farmhouse to Jack and sell the land. If only he could find someone to settle down with…' She laughed. 'Perhaps you know someone kind and lovely whom you could introduce Jack to!'

'I'll certainly be on the lookout,' murmured Frankie.

Jack was listening to them and groaned. 'Please, Mother! Don't ask Frankie to start matchmaking—these things never work out. Besides, I've just had one broken engagement—I think I'll give the marriage stakes a little rest for a while.'

Sheila shook her head impatiently. 'Really, Jack, she was such a nice girl—I can't imagine why you called it off. I really thought you were ready to settle down again.'

'I didn't feel she was the right person for me,' said Jack lightly.

'Tch! You men—always calling off engagements. You wouldn't see a perfect girl if there was one under your nose!' Sheila turned to Frankie. 'Don't you agree with me?'

'I think she'd tell me to wait until I meet the right person, wouldn't you Frankie?'

'Don't draw me into this discussion,' said Frankie. 'I only know that there must be plenty of girls longing for Jack to ask them out!' Privately she wished Sheila would move off the subject—it was obvious that Jack couldn't find anyone to match Sue.

There was another shrill whistle and the children got up and formed a line, each one being given a large spoon with a small plastic egg on it. When the race began, Abby walked very carefully with her tongue out, watching her egg fixedly, unaware that most of the others were running past her. But she kept doggedly on until she'd reached the finishing line. Frankie's heart went out to her when she saw the little girl look round to see the other racers and found they'd all finished ahead of her.

'I came last,' she said dolefully to her father, her mouth drooping.

'Sweetheart, you did brilliantly. You were the only one who didn't drop the egg for the whole race. I'm proud of you!' declared Jack, swinging her up in the air and kissing her.

What a great father he was, reflected Frankie, smiling at the little girl, who stared solemnly back at Frankie, suddenly shy of someone she hadn't seen for a while. Frankie bent down and gave her a kiss.

'You were great, Abby!' she exclaimed. 'You kept at it till the finishing line—we were all cheering you on.'

A voice over the Tannoy informed them that it was the parents' or childminders' race next, and asked everyone taking part to line up quickly. Abby looked up imploringly at Jack.

'Please, run in it…' she begged.

'I need a partner first,' said Jack. 'What about you, Frankie—or Mum?'

'Certainly not!' said Sheila. 'I'm not willing to end up with a twisted ankle. Frankie's young and fit!'

'I don't think I qualify.' Frankie laughed.

'Of course you do,' said Jack. He smiled down at her. 'You've certainly looked after Abby enough for me in the past.'

'Please, do,' implored Abby, twisting her hands together earnestly. 'Everyone else's mummy and daddy are going to be in it…'

'I'm not wearing the right gear,' protested Frankie, looking down at her layered cotton skirt.

'Nonsense,' said Jack, giving her a swift glance. 'You look very elegant—add a bit of style to the race.'

Abby's little face with her big brown eyes looked hopefully at Frankie, obviously wanting her family to be as much part of the proceedings as anyone else's. Frankie couldn't let her down.

'OK.' She smiled. 'I'm not the world's best athlete, though.'

To her dismay, the school had decided that the adults would have a three-legged race and a brisk woman handed out tape for each couple to bind their ankles together. Some of those parents who had come alone were put with other singles.

'Put your arms around each other's waists and put the bound feet forward first,' instructed the teacher bossily.

Jack's arm held Frankie's waist firmly and she put her arm around his muscled frame to support herself.

'Comfortable?' he asked her. 'If I'd known we were going to do this we should have practised.'

If she'd known they were going to be quite so intimately entwined, she didn't think she'd have come, reflected Frankie as they lined up at the starting line. She did her best to ignore the fluttering deep inside her and looked firmly ahead. What on earth would Jack think of her if he knew she was having these extraordinary reactions to him?

They waited for the woman to blow the starting whistle, Frankie's mind a jumble of conflicting emotions. She was lonely—that had to be it. Well, it would just have to stop!

The whistle blew and they started jerkily down the field, Jack's arm holding her so close to him that it was as if they were joined at the hip. Frankie could feel his strength as he practically carried her down the field, his heart thumping against her body.

Then she began to forget about the sensations running through her because it was fun, crazy, happy fun that she hadn't had for a long time. It made her giggle so much that she was helpless with laughter at the end of the race, catching hold of Jack when they stopped to prevent herself from falling over. He held her steady for a moment as she fell against him.

'Whoa! We've made it,' he said. He held her away from him for a second and looked down at her with dancing blue eyes. 'OK? No pulled ligaments?'

Frankie laughed breathlessly. 'I'm fine—but it's sure shown me I could do with a few workouts. I'm so unfit!'

Jack flicked an amused glance over her flushed cheeks and tousled hair springing round her head like a chestnut halo. 'You don't look unfit to me,' he murmured. 'Compared to the rest of the field, you're like an Olympic athlete!'

Frankie was still shaking with laughter when Abby and her grandparents came up to them.

'You won! You won!' shouted Abby, dancing around them in a frenzy of delight. She turned to her little friend and said proudly, 'My daddy and Frankie won—that makes them the best!'

'You certainly make a very good team,' remarked Brian, who had been sitting on a bench, resting his bad leg, as he watched them. 'If I hadn't had a gammy leg, Sheila and I would have had a go!'

'Next time I come to a school sports day I'll make sure I'm wearing a tracksuit,' declared Frankie.

'So you'll be coming to the one next year?' Jack's eyes

twinkled behind his glasses. 'In that case, we'd better get in some practice!'

Frankie wrinkled her nose at him. 'Don't push it, Jack. I don't feel the need to defend our title!'

They all laughed and Frankie suddenly thought that she hadn't enjoyed herself so much for months. There were some more races but then a few large drops of rain started to fall from the threatening skies, fast turning into a deluge of rain, and people started racing towards the car park.

'I thought this might happen sooner or later,' declared Sheila. 'We'd better get back to the farm now. Goodbye, my little angel.' She bent down to kiss her little granddaughter. 'I'll see you and Daddy tomorrow for lunch and you can help feed the new calf.' She turned to Frankie. 'It's been lovely to meet you. Please, come and see us at the farm some time.' She paused for a second and looked at Frankie with eyes as blue as her son's. 'And don't grieve after that man—I'd say you probably had a lucky escape!'

Frankie's hair was getting wetter by the minute, the umbrella she'd brought with her totally inadequate for the steady torrent of rain turning the field into a mudbath. There was a sudden flash of lightning and a few seconds later an ominous crack of thunder. Abby gave a shriek and clung to her father.

'Daddy, quick, the lightning's going to hit us. Let's go home!'

'OK, sweetheart. Don't worry—the storm's some way off yet. Hold my hand and we'll run.'

Abby gripped his hand and then took firm hold of Frankie's. 'Run with us, Frankie. Let's escape from the thunder,' she cried.

They began running across the field as the rain got harder

but when they got to the car park the place had already become a quagmire, with the cars churning up the mud.

'At least Mum's managed to get out before it got too bad,' said Jack. 'I wouldn't fancy trying to get their big heavy car out of something like this.' He stopped suddenly and pointed to Frankie's car. 'This is yours, isn't it? Looks like it's well bogged down in the mud.'

Frankie groaned. 'I just don't believe it.'

'I'll have a go at shifting it for you. Fortunately I'll have to reverse out, which gives the wheels a stronger grip.'

'For goodness' sake, Jack, you can't, not in this downpour. You take Abby and get off home.'

'Nonsense! Hold that umbrella over you both and I'll have a go—we're all wet anyway. I'll see if I can shift the car.'

There were cars revving up all round them, scattering mud in every direction as they tried to get out of the muddy car park. Frankie stepped carefully with Abby out of the way of one car slowly squelching past them, and at the same time Jack gave her car a terrific rev. The wheels spun round furiously and a spray of water and thick mud spattered liberally all over her.

What felt like a bowl of porridge hit her face and body. She gave a gasp of shock and then looked down at herself. The pretty flowered skirt she was wearing was soaked a dull brown and her T-shirt clung wetly to her. Abby seemed to have missed the worst of the onslaught. Frankie banged on the back of the car.

'For heaven's sake!' she yelled. 'Let Abby and me get out of the way!'

Abby's little face crinkled with laughter. 'Ooh, you're covered with mud. You look really funny!'

Sometimes, thought Frankie grimly, wiping her hand

across her mud-caked face, even the most attractive of children can be less than lovable. Jack peered at her, his face a picture of incredulity. Then he got out of the car and gazed helplessly at her, biting his lip to hide a surge of laughter.

'Er…I'm sorry,' he offered slowly.

'Sorry?' Frankie looked at him furiously. 'Why didn't you wait to see who was behind you? I couldn't move away until some of these cars had gone past.'

Jack looked contrite. 'I didn't see you, Frankie…I don't know what to say.'

'Well, what am I going to do now? I'm caked in mud and absolutely freezing.'

Jack stroked his chin thoughtfully. 'I think we'll leave your car here for a while until it's stopped raining. Come over to my house—it's very near the school—and let's get you cleaned up a bit.'

There didn't seem much else to do. Frankie marched beside him in silence, trying to ignore the curious and amused glances people gave her. Abby trotted by her side, still holding her hand. She looked anxiously up at her father and Frankie.

'Are you cross with Daddy?' she asked. 'Don't you like him any more?'

An amused glance passed between Frankie and Jack and she laughed. 'Of course I like your daddy. It was an accident and he was trying to get my car out of the mud. I just hope he never tries it again!'

They reached Jack's neat little cottage in a side road near the school and Jack opened the door. Frankie looked in dismay at the cream-coloured carpet that covered the hall and stairs.

'I can't come in here all covered with mud,' she said flatly.

'It's all right, Daddy will carry you up. That's what he does when I've got dirty feet,' Abby reassured her.

'A good idea,' agreed Jack. 'No need to worry.'

'No…no. I'm far too wet and smelly. You're clothes will be as muddy as mine,' protested Frankie in embarrassment.

'Daddy won't mind. Sometimes when I've been at Grandpa's farm I'm really smelly, too. He's used to it, aren't you, Daddy?'

'Of course I am. You go on up, Abby, and start the bath, and I'll carry Frankie up.'

Frankie opened her mouth to protest again, but Jack scooped her up effortlessly and carried her up the stairs to the bathroom. She was embarrassingly aware of the closeness of his chest to her, the resolute strength in his arms—it was useless to protest that he shouldn't carry her. He pushed the door of the bathroom open with his shoulder and put her down on the bath mat. Abby was opening a large bottle of bath salts and began shaking them liberally into the water.

'This will make it all nice and bubbly for you,' she explained.

'That's true,' agreed Frankie with a smile. She took the bottle away from Abby. 'That's lovely Abby, but I don't want bubbles up to the ceiling, you know!'

Abby giggled. 'Perhaps you'll disappear under them.' She laughed.

'You go down now, Abby. You can put on a DVD and I'll make some tea for us all.' Jack turned to Frankie. 'Take your things off and put them on this towel,' he said. 'Then I'll throw them into the washing machine.' He tossed her a towelling dressing-gown from the back of the door. 'Put this on and I'll have something hot for you when you come downstairs.'

Frankie gazed at herself in the full-length wall mirror and, despite herself, started to laugh. 'What a sight,' she murmured. 'Even my hair's full of mud.'

'I thought mud packs were supposed to be a good thing,' he said with a grin as he went out of the room.

Frankie sank into the hot bath and tilted her head back against the wall. What on earth was she doing in Jack's bath in the middle of a Saturday afternoon? The hot water lapped around her soothingly and suddenly soft classical music wafted through some speakers on the wall. There was a soft tap on the door and Jack's voice came through.

'Can I collect your clothes?' he asked. 'And if I close my eyes, will you take this drink to get your circulation going?'

Frankie opened her mouth to say 'Wait a minute,' but the door opened and an arm came round with a glass full of a golden liquid that looked inviting. She reached over, took the glass and sipped from it.

'Mmm—that's nice. What is it?'

'Whisky Mac,' Jack replied. 'Medically proven to help the circulation—hot water, tot of whisky and ginger wine...'

The arm scooped up Frankie's clothes from the floor and she could hear Jack going back down the stairs. She sipped some more and the hot water lapped deliciously around her. She felt more relaxed than she had for a long time. She started to drift off into a light doze, thinking about the fun she'd had with Jack and his family at the sports day. She relived the three-legged race she'd run with Jack, and in her dream she felt his body moving next to hers—muscular and athletic. They reached the end of the race and he was still holding her close to him as she caught her breath and looked up into his face. His expression was tender, faintly teasing.

'We make a good team, don't we, Frankie?' he murmured, tracing his finger down her jawline until it reached the little hollow spot on her neck and bending his head towards hers, hovering over her parted lips…

A hammering on the bathroom door made her wake with a start, the image of Jack's face fading and the steamy mirror on the wall opposite coming into focus. For a moment she wasn't sure what was reality and what was her dream, then with a feeling of guilt she realised that the main focus of her dream had been Jack.

'Are you OK?' Jack was shouting. 'You've been in there for ages. Come and have some tea.'

'I'm fine. Drifted off, I'm afraid.' Frankie splashed out of the bath hastily. 'I'll be down in a minute.'

She towelled herself roughly and rubbed her hair, then put on the big fluffy white dressing-gown that Jack had left for her. She mustn't stay long, she told herself sternly. As soon as Jack produced her dry clothes, she'd be off. Her dream had shaken her—she seemed unable to get the man out of her mind. She went downstairs and into the sitting room and Jack's voice floated through from the kitchen.

'Make yourself at home. I won't be a moment.'

The room was large and airy with a wide window looking over the garden. One half seemed to be dedicated to Abby's toys—a doll's house, a stack of books and a small chair with a teddy and a doll in it. The little girl herself was curled up on a chair, intently watching something on television. On a bookcase were several photographs—mostly of Abby, one poignantly of her holding her mother's hand, another with her grandparents.

Frankie looked at the last one on the shelf, a shock flickering through her when she saw that it showed a smiling Damian with Abby as a baby in his arms at the little girl's christening. He had a happy, tender smile on his face as he looked down at the baby, his thick blond hair blown in an attractive quiff over his forehead. Frankie felt a lump of emotion squeezing her throat. If things had gone to plan, they would have been married now—and perhaps they would have had their own child for him to hold.

A wave of unhappiness swept over her as she felt the uncertainty of a blank future, and the horrible resentment that she'd waited all this time for Damian, only to have her plans shattered in one letter. There was never going to be a future with Damian. She scrabbled in the pocket of the dressing-gown in vain to find a handkerchief to mop away the sudden tears that spilled out of her eyes. The enjoyment of the afternoon she'd just had was suddenly wiped away.

CHAPTER FOUR

'HERE WE ARE—hot tea and scones my mother made…' Jack came into the room and put a tray down on a small table. 'Shall I put some jam on the scone for you?'

'Fine.' Frankie's voice was slightly muffled. 'That would be lovely.'

Jack looked up, something in her voice catching his attention. 'You OK?'

'Of course.'

He frowned and stood up, going towards her with a cup of tea. 'Here—take this and I'll go and see if your clothes are dry.'

Frankie was forced to turn round and take the proffered cup. 'Thank you—that's great.'

Jack looked at her closely then took her arm and gently drew her into the kitchen with him. 'Have you been crying, Frankie? Something's wrong, isn't it?' He put a finger under her chin and tilted her head towards him. 'Are you upset about Damian?'

Frankie turned her face away from him abruptly, frightened that the kindness in his voice would really make her break down. 'I'm absolutely fine,' she said lightly, but feeling the hot tears welling up again at his sympathic voice. 'I'll just have this cup of tea quickly before I go home.'

'I don't believe you're fine. What's happened to upset you?'

She took Jack's proffered handkerchief and dabbed her eyes. 'It's stupid really. I saw that photo of Damian holding Abby at her christening. It made me remember just how long we'd been together…and I suppose I miss the…well, the idea of being with him, and what we might have had together.'

'It must be very hard for you.'

Something in his voice made her look up at him. 'Not as hard as it was for you Jack, when you lost Sue. You and she loved each other so much and you had a child together. At least,' she added drily, 'I'm the only one affected by our break-up.'

'Someone else will come along, I'm sure,' he said gruffly.

She laughed. 'I don't know about that. I was thirty when I met Damian. If I have to wait another thirty I'll be pushing it a bit to have a family!'

He took his glasses off and polished them absent-mindedly with his handkerchief. 'I guess…' he said at last, an odd little quirk lifting his lips. 'I guess I would wait for ever for that special someone.'

Frankie forgot her own sadness and looked at him impishly. 'I personally know a super girl who would suit you down to the ground. She's told me she'd love to get to know you better.'

Frankie thought of Corey, longing for a man and definitely attracted to Jack. She would make a lovely wife.

Jack looked at her quizzically. 'You think I need someone, do you?'

'Well…I know how lonely you must be. We've talked about that before—being on your own isn't much fun.'

'I did try to rectify that only a short time ago,' he reminded her. 'It didn't work.'

Frankie looked earnestly at him. 'Why not let me try and arrange a date for you?'

His hand went out to touch a wet strand of hair that had fallen over her brow, then his finger traced a line under her chin and down her neck, a faint smile on his lips. Frankie tensed at his touch—it was practically a re-run of the dream she'd had in the bath…

'You're so kind, Frankie,' he sighed. 'Such a good friend—but no. I…I think I know the kind of person I need—so don't bother your friend.'

From that Frankie gathered that it was too soon for him to fall in love again. It was still Sue who filled his heart and no one was going to live up to her at the moment. She smiled at him.

'I understand, Jack. I'll keep it on hold.'

'Thank you for that. Who knows? One day I may find someone myself—but you know how grateful I am for your concern.'

He bent towards her and brushed her forehead in a light kiss, then stepped back and smiled back at her with those cobalt blue eyes. Frankie vaguely heard the television booming out a children's song in the other room, but inside the kitchen the atmosphere suddenly became rather intimate, quiet and still, as if something momentous was going to happen. She felt an overwhelming fondness for this man who had acted as a kind of bridge between her and Damian, never talking of his own difficulties and listening so patiently to hers. Before she knew what she was doing, she put one arm round his neck and drew his face down to hers, her lips pressing softly against his cheek. She wanted to show how much she appreciated his compassion—that was all, wasn't it?

'We must look out for each other,' she whispered.

He gave a quick intake of breath and hugged her in return, his arm encircling her waist and pulling her to him so that her soft body was held fast to his muscular frame. Frankie forgot about her plans to keep her distance from him—all she could think of was the solid feel of his body against hers and how comforting it was. Somewhere at the back of her mind floated the thought that she shouldn't be cuddling up to Jack like this, and then she almost laughed out loud. She was a free agent now, wasn't she? She could do what she liked….

Perhaps Jack was thinking of that, too, for he sighed and pushed her away gently, looking down at her with a wry humour in his eyes. 'Damian doesn't know what he's thrown away,' he said lightly, as he turned away and briskly started to set out mugs and plates on a tray.

Frankie's cheeks flamed with embarrassment and she bit her lip, an ominous emotion snaking treacherously through her—the feeling that she hadn't wanted him to stop, that what they had started she wanted them to finish…

'Please, can I have some cake Daddy?'

Abby's clear little voice cut through the silence of her embarrassment and they turned round to see her standing in the doorway. She looked at them both crossly.

'What are you two doing? You've been ages and *ages,* and I've been waiting for my tea all this time!'

Frankie and Jack looked at each other guiltily, then he grinned, the tension between them broken by the child's voice.

'Sorry, sweetheart,' he said. 'I was trying to tell Frankie that we'd always be here if she needed our help.'

He replaced his glasses and ran a hand through his hair so that it stood up spikily on his head. 'I think we could all do with a scone now, couldn't we?'

Frankie was silent. She went into the living room and sat down on the sofa, her legs feeling unable to hold her up. What on earth had come over her just then? How could she have deliberately pulled Jack towards her and practically offered herself to him? The thing was, she thought dazedly, it had all been tantalisingly and teasingly filled with the most delicious promise of things that might have been—and that to her astonishment she wished had been carried further! What a good job they had stopped before she had embarrassed both of them…

Sunday, one a.m. Only six more hours to go, reflected Frankie, flicking a look at her watch as she sat at one of the computers, trying to bring up urgent notes on a heart patient who'd been taken onto the cardiac unit. It had been the usual bedlam of a Saturday night, with several drunks in who'd been involved in a fight and who had injuries ranging from minor cuts and bruises to quite serious head wounds. And then there were the breakages…people playing football and rugby regularly seemed to snap limbs or damage cartilage on a Saturday afternoon but usually waited until the evening before they decided their injury was serious enough to need hospital attention. She glanced up at the whiteboard on the wall above the desk and could see that three more patients had been written up during the last few minutes. Par for the course— Saturday night building up to a climax.

Despite the rush and turmoil of the department, Frankie enjoyed it—the buzz, the variety of people and injuries. No night was ever the same. She'd started doing nights at the beginning of the week and it had been quite a relief. At least Jack wasn't on the same shift as her and she could start to relax, put things into perspective about her feelings for him. She wasn't attracted to him as such, she told herself sternly. It was purely the association of him with Damian that made her *think* she was, and in consequence that was why Jack kept springing into her mind when there was a lull at work. Nevertheless, she conceded, it was a situation that could escalate into something that teetered on the edge of danger.

From now on she would keep her distance from Jack and try to avoid working on his shift as much as possible. And that was why there was no way she was going to ask him to come with her to the special evening where her father was being made Vice Chancellor of Denniston University and afterwards to the ball to honour the occasion. Her parents particularly wanted her to be there, and had told her if Damian couldn't be there to find a friend to partner her for the evening. She made a face at the thought—it would be better to turn up by herself. As it was, she really must tell them that her engagement was over…

A loud aggressive voice floated down the corridor, cutting across her thoughts. 'When the hell will we be seen, then?'

Frankie looked up from the desk and saw a thickset man in a dark suit, stabbing the air with his index finger in front of Sister Kenney and an apprehensive-looking Cindy standing by her side. He made an incongruously stylish figure among the bedraggled patients and their friends waiting in the reception area. His voice became louder.

'Do you know who you've got in that cubicle? Only Denver Clayton, that's all! Surely to God you know who he is?'

'Mr Clayton's only just been brought into the department. A triage nurse will have assessed him as to the severity of his condition.' Sister Kenney's tone was firm but polite. 'I assure you that he will be seen as soon as possible.'

'I should damn well think so,' said the aggressive man. 'That nurse you talked about only looked a kid—we need someone professional on the job.'

'We are all professionals here,' remarked Sister Kenney, a touch of ice in her tone. She wasn't going to be bullied. She went up to Frankie and murmured in her ear. 'This gentleman's friend is in cubicle three—he seems rather disorientated. He collapsed in town about half an hour ago, but he's coming round a bit now.'

Frankie eyes met Sister Kenney's in a flicker of amused exasperation for a fraction of a second. Not that Frankie was surprised by the man's attitude—it happened on a daily basis. She sympathised with the relatives and friends of patients who were oblivious to what was happening in the rest of the unit, but it didn't excuse the aggressive and pugnacious behaviour of what seemed to be the majority on a Saturday night—most of them, like this man, fuelled in his aggression by alcohol.

She went into the cubicle and looked at the patient lying on the bed. He wasn't very old, thirtyish, Frankie guessed, with spiked hair dyed alternatively black and white at the front. His face seemed vaguely familiar. He wore a T-shirt with I AM THE MUSIC printed in large letters across it and faded ripped jeans. He moaned occasionally and shifted restlessly on the bed, his eyes closed, his breathing rather laboured.

'Better give him some oxygen,' said Frankie to Cindy, who had followed her into the room. 'Slip that oxygen mask over his face, will you?'

Cindy started to do as she was asked, then stood back, staring reverently at the patient, her eyes wide. 'Denver Clayton,' she breathed. 'Just to think, I saw him on stage only ten days ago,' she added in a stage whisper to Frankie.

Frankie put her stethoscope on his chest and listened to his heart. 'Palpitating a bit, but it does seem to be slowing down,' she murmured, then removed her stethoscope from her ears. 'Is he a singer?' she enquired.

Cindy looked at her in amazement. 'He's only the lead singer in the Music Bones—everyone knows him!'

She must be getting old, thought Frankie and she was definitely not getting out enough if everyone seemed to know this guy but her!

'I thought his face was vaguely familiar,' she said. 'Stay with Mr Clayton while I talk to his friend about what happened.'

Frankie went out of the cubicle where the belligerent friend and a young girl with thick blonde hair tied up in a tangled knot on top of her head and a minute leopard-print skirt were waiting.

'Are you friends or relatives of Mr Clayton's?' asked Frankie.

'I'm Bill Courtney, Denver's manager.' The man gestured to the girl by his side. 'This is Vicky, Denver's girlfriend.'

'His fiancée,' corrected the girl quickly.

'Were you with him when he became ill?'

'Yeah,' replied the man. 'Give us all a fright, he did. Starts gasping and banging at his chest—eyes streaming and then drops like a stone. Bloody frightening it was. We'd just done a gig in town and he was on a high—fit as a flea.'

Vicky began to cry, snivelling softly into a handkerchief. 'He did really great tonight—standing ovation. It was horrible when he just collapsed like that with no warning.'

'Had he taken anything?'

The man scowled, looking pugnaciously at Frankie. 'Just because he's a pop star doesn't mean he does drugs. He's not into that scene, see? He's a favourite of all the mums and they won't like it if they think he's not on the straight and narrow. Anyone who says he's taking something, we'll sue them for defamation of character.'

'That's what they'll all say,' wailed Vicky. 'But it's not true…'

'Look,' said Frankie patiently, 'I'm only trying to diagnose what's happened to your friend. Anything you say to me is in the strictest confidence. If you say he never takes drugs, that's fine. Did he have anything to drink?'

Bill shrugged. 'Sure. We always have a few after the performance. Helps to wind you down, relax you, see?'

For 'few drinks' read 'gallons' thought Frankie, recognising the florid and sweating complexion of someone who'd had plenty of alcohol in Bill.

'And how long ago did this happen?' she asked.

'About half an hour ago now. We'd just been to the Chinese place round the corner from the theatre. They stay open late and we'd not had anything all evening, so they heated something up for us.'

'I see. Well perhaps you would wait in the side corridor where there are some chairs and a drinks machine while we attend to Mr Clayton.'

'And how long's that going to take?' demanded Bill in his loud, hectoring way, thrusting his face towards Frankie. 'We want some answers soon. We've got another gig tomorrow night in Manchester. Can't afford to let the punters down.'

Frankie wished she was another six inches taller—it would be nice to look down on this unpleasant man instead of having him tower over her. She saw the man shift his gaze beyond her and a deep familiar voice said smoothly over her shoulder, 'What's going on? Something the matter?'

It was a shock to realise that Jack was on night duty after all, but a feeling of relief went through her. She knew from experience that Jack was not a man to be bullied and it was nice to have back-up when trying to deal with someone like Bill Courtney.

'Mr Courtney is a friend of the patient in cubicle three, a Mr Denver Clayton. I'm just getting some background information,' she explained.

Jack's eyes glinted coldly behind his glasses and he looked down stonily at the burly figure of Bill. Jack looked quite a strapping figure, tall and athletic in comparison to Denver Clayton's manager.

'So, Mr Courtney, what exactly is your worry?' His voice was courteous but steely. 'We need to know what happened and we don't want to rush to conclusions. I'm sure you wouldn't want us to do that.'

Bill shuffled slightly under Jack's authoritarian manner. 'They don't seem to know what the hell's the matter with him. I thought that was what your training was for…'

'I suggest you do as Dr. Lovatt said and go and get a coffee from the machine in the corridor, leaving us, as you say, to do our jobs. Let's go and look at the patient, Dr. Lovatt.'

Vicky took Bill's arm and pulled him towards the waiting area. 'Let's have something to drink—I'm parched. Have you got any change? We'll have to leave it to them.'

'The young girl's got more sense than the man,' remarked Jack as he and Frankie went into the cubicle.

They looked down at Denver's ashen face and Frankie said thoughtfully, 'I've had an idea…I might be wrong because I've only heard of this and not actually encountered it…'

'Go ahead,' said Jack, as he palpated the man's abdomen and then felt for the pulse on his wrist.

'Well, he's just had a Chinese meal on top of a substantial amount of alcohol. Apparently the restaurant heated some up for his party as they were so late. I wondered if he was suffering from a reaction to monosodium glutamate?'

'Sounds feasible,' agreed Jack. 'They call it Chinese restaurant syndrome.' He put his hand on the man's jaw and nodded. 'He's very hot—I believe that's a symptom. He's certainly coming round now—quite stable.'

'Probably all he needs is time to recover and then a nice big mug of black coffee.'

Cindy's eyes were round with interest. 'Well, I never. Could put you off Chinese food couldn't it?' she exclaimed. 'I'm always having Chinese take-aways.'

Jack grinned. 'I don't think you've any need to worry. Just don't drink loads of alcohol before you eat it—and remember that reheating it in a microwave concentrates the monosodium glutamate. Would you go and get Mr Clayton's friends? I think we've got the answer to his problem.'

Vicky and Bill pushed their way into the cubicle and stared gloomily at the patient still lying with his eyes closed on the bed.

'Is he no better, then?' asked Bill.

'Certainly he is,' said Frankie briskly. 'His breathing and pulse are fine now. I think he's just sleeping off the excesses of the evening.'

'If the press get hold of this they'll have it all over that he's been taking stuff,' Bill said glumly. 'We'll never hear the end of it—and bang goes our family reputation.'

'He could be fine in about half an hour,' said Frankie. 'We'll give him some coffee when he's come round properly and he'll be none the worse tomorrow.'

Vicky turned big blue eyes framed by thick black mascara on Frankie. 'We're getting married soon,' she said shyly. 'I couldn't bear anything to happen to him.'

Frankie smiled at her. She was so young, and there was something sweet and naive about her. 'He's lucky that he's got someone like you to look after him,' she said kindly.

'Well, what the hell's been the matter with him anyway?' asked Bill.

'He's had a reaction to the chemical monosodium glutamate that's added to flavour some Chinese food,' explained Jack. 'It is unusual and he should be fine soon.'

As if on cue, Denver moaned and then sat up rather groggily. 'Hell, I feel rough. What am I doing here?'

He looked around the cubicle in a bewildered way and Vicky gave a little scream of delight and hugged him. 'Oh, babe, you're OK! You had us really worried then. You passed out…'

'No more Chinese food for you when we're on tour,' growled Bill. 'And I'm going to wait in the car. I'm bushed!'

Frankie turned to Vicky. 'Perhaps you'd stay with your

fiancé for a while. We'll come back in half an hour and check on his progress. If he's improved we can discharge him.'

Vicky's tired little face beamed. 'That's great. Hear that, babe? You can go home soon.'

'I didn't know you were on nights,' said Frankie as she and Jack walked back towards the central nurses' station, where Sister Kenney was updating the names of patients on the whiteboard and noting to what cubicles they'd been assigned.

'I'm not really,' replied Jack. 'Just standing in for Pete Jones, who has flu.' He yawned. 'I don't know about you, but I could do with some caffeine intravenously—I've been on duty since one o'clock yesterday.'

Frankie remembered her decision to distance herself from Jack. 'I've got a load of paperwork to do,' she said lightly. 'I'll have some later.'

'Well, it's quiet enough now,' remarked Sister Kenney. 'I should grab some coffee while you can.'

There was a general air of relaxation as the unit seemed to pause in the lull between patients. Tim, the genial porter, was tightening the valves on some oxygen cylinders, humming in a deep melodious voice to himself. Corey was poring over her horoscope in one of the lurid daily papers someone had left in the waiting room, and Frankie could hear Cindy telling the receptionist in a hushed voice about meeting Denver Clayton.

'Sure I can't tempt you?' said Jack. 'I really want to thank you for coming to Abby's sports day—she was so thrilled. I've got a photo, by the way.' He held it out to Frankie. 'My father took it of you and I winning the carers' and parents' race.' He grinned. 'You look as if you're enjoying it.'

Frankie grimaced. She certainly looked happy, laughing up

at Jack as he lifted her over the finishing line, but her skirt was whipped up around her thighs, revealing just how long her legs were, and her cleavage was rather obvious as she'd bent forward over Jack's arm.

'Not exactly flattering,' she murmured.

'I think it shows you off to definite advantage,' Jack teased. 'Anyway, it's a reminder of a good afternoon.'

An afternoon that had ended up a little too intimately, reflected Frankie, and the reason she wasn't going to do anything that meant she and Jack were alone together.

'I don't think there'll be time for a coffee,' she said firmly. As if on cue, the standby phone suddenly sprang into life. She gave a half-smile and said, 'I didn't know it would ring—honest!' as she lifted it with an apologetic shrug.

'Hello. Denniston Vale A and E. Dr. Lovatt here.' Her eyes narrowed as she listened and made notes on a pad of paper. 'Yes, got that. Elderly male fallen at home, aged about 87 years—probable heart attack. His wife injured as well. May have broken collar-bone. OK…'

She put the phone down and stood up briskly. 'You heard that, everyone? ETA of these patients about five minutes. Jack, ring CCU and warn them we may have someone coming after we've assessed this patient.'

The tension in the unit suddenly racheted up a notch and those staff not involved with other patients made their way to the majors area where the recussitation unit was situated by the main ambulance entrance. It was as if a general surge of adrenalin went through the team and a longing for coffee or to put one's feet up was forgotten in the general feeling of anticipation.

'This is Mr Ben Stoneham—he looks bad,' murmured Tim as he wheeled the elderly man into the resus room a few minutes later.

'What happened?' asked Jack, his fingers on the man's wrist, noting the white pallor and sheen of perspiration on Mr Stoneham's forehead.

'His wife fell getting out of bed and he collapsed when he tried to help her get up,' said Tim. 'They're lucky. He had one of those discs round his neck so his wife got help that way.'

'Good job they had that,' murmured Jack. 'His pulse is pretty weak,' he said to Frankie. 'Better get a longer airway in than this one…'

As Frankie was changing the airways there was a sudden gurgling sound and the man's veins became prominent in his neck as his body struggled to get breath and his face turned a deep purple. Frankie swore softly and looked up at Jack.

'Hit the button, Jack, he's arresting!'

Jack smacked the cardiac button by the door of the unit and within seconds of the squeal of the alarm Corey and Sister Kenney had joined Jack and Frankie. They slipped into the co-ordination of a medical team, aware that speed was the essential in the first stages of acute cardiac failure, one nurse unrolling the pack of injectible drugs that provided a life support for a heart-attack victim until he could be transferred to the specialist cardiac unit, another hooking the man up to the cardiac trace to monitor his heart.

'We need bloods—and what's his drug situation?' asked Frankie, watching the oximeter, which was giving a continuous reading of blood pressure and oxygen levels. Above his head the electronic trace of his erratic heartbeat was spidering its way across the graph, the sound of its blips nothing like the reassuring pattern it should have been.

'Three hundred milligrams aspirin administered in the ambulance. Streptokinase administered on arrival in unit,' Sister Kenney informed them.

'BP's slightly better—80 over 55, oxygen sats 85, heartbeat 110,' said Frankie after a few seconds.

There was a short silence as everybody waited to see if the improvement was maintained, then Jack gave a slight smile of satisfaction. 'Ah—I think he's settling back into sinus rhythm, folks.' His eyes were fixed on the trace as he continued to listen to the man's chest. 'Great. He's back with us again.'

The blips began to calm down, sounding more like the constant drip of a tap than the scary rapid tattoo they'd been giving.

'CCU are waiting for him so he can be taken down now. Keep the oxygen up,' said Frankie as she finished drawing off some blood from the patient's arm. 'I'll send these bloods down, too.'

As Tim started to wheel Mr Stoneham away, the old man's eyes fluttered open and his arm went out to touch Frankie as he passed her.

'Where's my Gladys?' he whispered.

Frankie bent down. 'Don't worry,' she assured him. 'Mrs Stoneham's in the cubicle down the corridor. I checked with the nurse, she's had an X-ray and we've found she's got a broken collar-bone—very painful, but not too serious. We're keeping her in for the night and we'll wheel her in to see you in the morning.'

'Tell her not to come until she's bought me baccy and that

whisky I keep in the sideboard—see?' He looked as fiercely as he could at Frankie from behind his oxygen mask. 'And I mean it, too. I need spoiling now!'

There was sudden lightening of the tense atmosphere in the room. The team had saved an old man who had been close to death and as Corey said when the patient had gone, 'It was lovely to hear Mr Stoneham being cheeky!'

And that was the upside of Casualty, thought Frankie, the genuine happiness of the team when they'd managed to save a patient close to death. She walked quickly to the examination area where the triage nurse had asked her to come and see a patient. Frankie groaned inwardly when she saw who it was. Colin Burroughs was a 'multiple attender' at A and E, each time protesting that he had serious problems and demanding that he be admitted for the night for investigations. After exhaustive tests nothing was ever found, and he would be sent home.

Frankie could see him sitting in a corner of the room, looking chirpily through rheumy eyes at a hospital leaflet. His shabby old mac was tied round his waist with string and he wore old trainers with holes cut in them to allow his bunions to peep out. A large supermarket bag stuffed with papers lay at his feet. All the staff knew that what he wanted was a bed for the night and some food, and, as Sister Kenney remarked, 'a jolly good bath'.

The triage nurse took Frankie to one side. 'Mr Burroughs is going to be difficult to shift tonight,' she said.

'Why, what's he got wrong with him this time?' asked Frankie.

'Says he'll top himself if we don't admit him,' she said succinctly.

'That's a difficult one,' agreed Frankie. 'You can't have a scan to prove he's suicidal—he certainly looks happy enough.'

She went and stood by the man. 'Hello, Mr Burroughs. How are you this evening?'

'Rotten,' he said cheerfully. 'I'm going to kill myself.'

Frankie sat down by him and smiled. 'You aren't really going to do that, are you?'

He scowled. 'I'm at the end of my tether. If you don't get me in here for the night, I'll do something foolish.'

He looked at her craftily. He'd hit on something she couldn't prove and daren't ignore. But there was something pitiful about him. Frankie wondered what had happened to bring him to this state. He must have been a fine figure of a man at some time— now he looked a shambles, uncared-for, unkempt, unloved.

'Would you like a cup of tea and we'll have a talk about it?'

He smiled, a toothless grin. 'Yep—hot, mind, and plenty of sugar.'

Frankie began to ask him about his general health, and after a few minutes when he'd expounded on the things that must have made his life very uncomfortable, from his rheumatics to his piles, she said gently, 'These are all things we can give you medicine for, but are you sure you really want to come into hospital. Are you honestly feeling suicidal?'

He sighed and pulled at his beard. 'I suppose not,' he mumbled. Then, with a burst of honesty, he said, 'What I want is a permanent place in a hostel. Life on the streets isn't much fun when you're my age. If you was to write a note to the council saying I'm on the streets they'd take notice of you, see? One night here and there is no good to me now—I need something more steady.'

'I'll see that's done,' agreed Frankie. 'I'll ask the consultant who's in tomorrow to write one—you just give all your particulars to the receptionist.'

And that was all it took to make an old man very happy, thought Frankie as she watched Mr Burroughs whistle his way down the corridor, having achieved his objective.

Nearly time to go home. Frankie caught sight of herself in the mirror of the staff kitchen and grimaced. The night had taken its toll, and now she longed for a hot bath and a long, refreshing sleep.

She'd made a decision during the night, brought on partly by her desire to keep away from Jack. She'd managed to get some holiday time in three weeks and she would book a flight to Brazil and make her own way to the island where Damian was. She didn't care if it was a danger zone—she wouldn't rest until she'd met the man face to face and demanded that he tell her just why he'd finished with her. They'd been engaged for a long time and although he'd said that it would be dangerous for her to visit him there, there'd never been an inkling that he wanted to split up. Until she found out, she felt she couldn't draw a line under the past—and she couldn't concentrate on her future.

She leaned back in the chair, feeling good that she'd come to a firm decision about facing Damian. She picked up one of the early morning papers that one of the consultants had left on the table and ran her eye down the society column, amused at some of the stories about the celebrities' love lives that seemed to make up most of the article. She didn't notice the photograph at first—it was of a couple of people at some star-studded gathering. The caption read, 'Betsy St John, on location filming her latest blockbuster, is engaged! The wedding will be in June and here she celebrates with her new love on the beach of a romantic island off South America.'

Frankie gave the photo a cursory glance, then frowned and looked more closely, her face paling slightly.

'What the hell?' she said to the empty room, her eyes travelling disbelievingly over the image. Then her mouth went dry and her heart thumped uncomfortably against her ribs. The photo was very clear—it was of Betsy St John gazing adoringly up at Damian, her body pressed to his. There was no mistaking that it was Damian for his face was turned fully to the camera, that good-looking, boyish face with a thick quiff of fair hair and a wide triumphant smile on his lips.

'So that was the reason he left me—and he didn't have the guts to explain,' she whispered.

CHAPTER FIVE

IT WAS UNBELIEVABLE. Frankie began to read the article below the picture, her hands shaking a little with the shock.

'Betsy St John, able to command a million dollars a film, is to marry Damian Montrose, chairman of a small clothing factory on a tiny island off Brazil. She met him while on location for her latest film and according to both of them, it was "love at first sight"'.

'"He is everything I need in a man,"' gushed Betsy. '"He knows how to treat a girl well. He may not be in show business but he sure looks the part!"'

'Oh, for God's sake!' Frankie almost shouted the words. 'Knows how to treat a girl, indeed! What a fool I've been…'

Damian was a liar, wasn't he? Out for what he could get, sweet-talking her into believing that she shouldn't come over and see him. What was the excuse he'd given? That it would be dangerous for her. And she had believed him! Then he had said he would always love her and when he returned at the end of a year, if she still wanted him, they would get married. She shrugged, reflecting that he had said so many things— and probably all of them were lies.

It was as if someone had wiped a misty mirror in front of her and all had become perfectly clear. Frankie got up and began to pace the floor, trying to calm herself, to come to terms with the fact that now Damian belonged to someone else. Betsy St John would have the benefit of his lively wit, his knack of making you feel that you were the only one he wanted to be with and listen to…. Ha! That was all an act, she knew that now. Perhaps she'd suspected it for some time, but hadn't liked to admit to herself that she'd been in love with a womaniser. She thought with self-disgust that she'd believed all his honeyed words and flattery. More fool her.

She screwed the newspaper up into a ball and threw it into the wastepaper basket. No doubt people would read about it soon and she would be the laughing stock of those who knew her—or, even worse, the object of their pity…

'Are you off home, then, or do you want to stay here all day as well?' Corey was standing in front of Frankie, looking quizzically at her. 'You OK? You look as if you've seen a ghost,' she added, stooping down to pick up some dirty mugs from the table.

Frankie pulled the paper out of the wastepaper basket and smoothed it out, thrusting it in front of Corey. 'Look at this,' she said grimly. 'I've just realised that I've been an absolute idiot, that's all.'

Corey's eyes scanned the article Frankie held in front of her and she gave a low whistle. 'Hell—so that's what he's been up to! Why couldn't he have told you?'

'Because he's a coward, that's why. I've been wearing blinkers, haven't I?' Frankie got up. 'Let's go,' she said brusquely. 'I'm longing for a hot bath.'

'Never mind, sweetheart, he's not worth worrying about. How he could choose someone like that plastic doll over you I don't know,' said Corey soothingly. She put an arm round Frankie's shoulders and hugged her. 'And a hot bath will do you a world of good—I've been thinking of that very thing for about two hours now!'

They went to the locker-room to pick up their bags and then went out to the car park. Frankie waved goodbye to Corey but when she got into her car she slammed the door with the force of a terrible anger. To think she'd said she'd wait for ever to marry Damian, that she'd thought what an altruistic man he was, thinking only of her and of keeping his business going. She ground the gears fiercely as she roared out of the car park, scattering stones behind her. At the moment her emotions were mainly fury and a feeling of shame that she'd been so easy to dupe.

The answering machine was blinking when she arrived back home and when she pressed the 'play' button her mother's voice floated over the room.

'Hello, darling, just to remind you that we look forward to seeing you next week at the university ball. We'll send a car for you to meet us at the university and we'll all have a drink. There'll be lots of hospital people there so you'll probably know plenty of them. From what you said, Damian's still abroad, trying to sort out his business problems, so we've asked one of Dad's younger colleagues to come along to make up the numbers. Speak to you soon.'

Frankie groaned as she erased the message. She didn't relish telling her parents about Damian, but it would have to be done. Chances were, they would see the story in the papers later that day. From now on, she thought despondently, she would have to get used to being single. Then she gave herself a mental shake. The evening was going to be a great honour for her beloved father and she didn't want anything to spoil it, so she would look as if she was enjoying it even if it meant hours of tedium with an unknown man!

She picked up a photograph of herself and Damian in her parents' garden taken eighteen months before. The sun was shining and he was holding her close to him—in a pose reminiscent of the photograph in the paper, she reflected painfully. On the right of the picture were Jack and Sue, smiling in pleasure at their happiness, self-effacing, never the centre of the crowd. How very different the two men were, Frankie reflected sadly. She could not imagine Jack ever conning anyone.

With a coldly deliberate action Frankie drew her arm back and with all the force she could muster she flung the photo viciously into the fireplace, the glass shattering all over the carpet. Then she took some letters that had been on the table and shredded them savagely, throwing the pieces on the floor. And for a second she felt rather better about his public dumping of her.

'You complete rat,' she whispered.

She began to pace up and down the room, her blood boiling with anger that she should have been so blind. The signs had all been there—the excuses Damian had given for not coming home to see her, the reasons he hadn't wanted her to go and see him. With hindsight they'd all been suspect. And yet…and yet they'd had such fun together. Damian loved parties and socialising and wherever he was there seemed to be laughter. But that meant nothing now, she thought fiercely, and she would push it to the back of her mind.

She got up from her chair to look out of the window to the parkland beyond. It was going to be a lovely day—the sun was up and the trees had that fresh greenness about them that could only happen in the spring. She opened the window and watched the people crossing the park, children, old men and women, cyclists... The world was going on quite happily and she must move on too. Through the window the air felt fresh and invigorating—and it seemed to reflect her mood of renewal and determination to get on with her life.

She was free now, she thought. She didn't need a man to make her life complete—certainly not a rat like Damian!

She jumped as the doorbell pealed stridently—who would be coming to see her this early on a Sunday morning? She opened the door and looked in surprise at Jack standing on the doorstep—he was the last person she'd expected to see.

'What...what are you doing here?' she asked. 'I'd have thought after night duty you'd have been wending your way home by now.'

'Can I come in?' he said abruptly. His expression was very serious and suddenly Frankie knew why he had come. She stood aside and he went into the sitting room, with her following. His eyes flickered round the room, taking in the broken picture frame and the torn paper, which told their own story.

'I guess you know about Damian,' he said quietly. 'I was coming to tell you.'

Frankie stood and faced him, her arms folded. 'Did you see it in the paper?' she asked flatly.

'On the early morning news. I had to see a patient on the ward and he had his bedside television on.'

Frankie groaned. 'So all the world will know now.' She tipped her chin up and stared at Jack defiantly. 'So what? I saw his photo in a tabloid so I guess it's common knowledge now. For all I know, I'm the last to hear about Damian's bloody engagement. I've been a perfect fool—so naive it isn't true. If only I'd known…'

'I'm so sorry Frankie.'

'Don't be!' she said vehemently. 'You know something? It may seem extraordinary, but I don't care. All I know is I've wasted a year of my life being besotted with someone who wasn't worth my loyalty. Now I'm free and I'm damn well going to make the most of it—not be tied down to anyone again for a long time!'

He laughed, raising his eyebrows in surprise. 'Good for you. I didn't think you'd be quite so positive about it all.' He looked at her perceptively and his voice was gentle. 'You must surely still have some feelings for him—you can't just switch off like that.'

Frankie looked down at her hands and nodded a little bleakly. 'I suppose that's true. I went out with him for a long time and it leaves a gap, of course it does. It's hard to believe that he's not mine any more.'

Her eyes were bright with unshed tears and she bit her lip to hold them back.

'I know, Frankie.'

'It's not nice to find out you've been abandoned. Oh, I knew he was very attractive to women. He only had to walk into a room and every girl there would follow him with their eyes.'

'That's true,' acknowledged Jack. 'And I think he was aware of it.'

Frankie frowned. 'Did you know what was going on?'

Jack looked uncomfortable. 'I did have my suspicions.'

She stared at him wordlessly for a second, then she said incredulously, 'You had your suspicions all the months when we worked with each other? Then why didn't you tell me? You allowed me to go on thinking he loved me and yet—'

Jack put his hand up as if to stem the tide of words. 'Look, if I had, would you have believed me? I had no concrete evidence for my suspicions—just the way he talked about other women. But he always said he was mad about you and that he looked forward to coming back to England and getting married.'

Frankie moved nearer to him and put her hands on her hips, looking at him belligerently. 'I suppose you were just protecting your precious friend. Well, don't forget I was a friend of yours too!'

He leant forward and brushed away a lock of hair from her forehead, saying gently, 'I hope you still are a friend, Frankie. I couldn't bear to lose that friendship.'

Frankie bit her lip, trying not to let the bitterness show in her voice. 'You didn't seem too bothered when you left St Mary's without a word of explanation.'

A closed expression flickered across his face. 'I will explain,' he said slowly. 'One day, I promise. It wouldn't be appropriate at the moment…but I can't begin to tell you how angry I am that he's hurt you.'

She shook her head impatiently. 'It isn't just me for God's sake. My father funded Damian to secure the land the factory was on. I doubt if that money will ever be repaid. How can I live with myself for causing my parents any worry?'

Jack shook his head. 'It wasn't your fault—you believed everything Damian said because you trust people and he has a silver tongue. He fooled me and I've known him since childhood—and don't forget, he's my brother-in-law. He and Sue had very different characters, but she adored him, and whatever he's done he has charisma and verve.'

'Oh, he's got that all right,' Frankie said bitterly. 'But I'm a fool, too. It'll be a long time before I commit myself to anybody again.'

He gave a wry little smile. 'You say that now…'

'And I mean it,' she replied fiercely. 'I'm not going to throw away my freedom so easily again. Damian dangled me on a string to get backing for his wretched family business. Now he can get his hands on Betsy St John's mega-bucks he doesn't need me.'

'To be honest,' Jack said slowly, 'I can hardly believe it of Damian. He's a flirt, yes, he loves to be the centre of attention, but I would never have believed he could be so cruel.'

'He's shown he doesn't give a damn for me or my feelings,' Frankie remarked flatly.

'When he realises what he's done, he may regret it.'

'He can regret all he likes—I'm going to get on with my life now. Instead of waiting around for Damian, I'm going to start pursuing a worthwhile career. I've been treading water at the hospital for too long while he's been cheating on me.'

'Quite right! You've got the talent to do anything you want.'

Jack moved forward and put his hands on her shoulders. 'Look, if I'd had definite proof that Damian was two-timing you, I would have told you.'

The touch of his hands sent a tremor through Frankie, and a mixture of sadness and anger brought a horrible lump to her throat. 'You men—you always stick together,' she said tightly. 'Why don't you admit that Damian is a rat? Just because he was your wife's brother, why couldn't you have just come out with your suspicions, instead of leaving me to find out by myself? You're just as phoney as he is!'

The lump in her throat translated into enormous tears that spilled out of her eyes and tearing sobs that shook her body. Without a word Jack pulled her towards him and put his arms around her, rocking her like a young child against his chest, stroking the back of her neck and putting his cheek against hers until her crying had calmed down and she remained still against him. Gently he turned her head towards his and looked down at her with those intense blue eyes, so close to her she could see the black lashes that fringed them.

'Feeling better?' he asked gently.

'Thank you, yes,' she whispered, feeling the reassuring thump of his heart against hers, the strength of his powerful frame supporting her. 'I…I'm sorry. I shouldn't have accused you of lying…or being as bad as Damian.'

His arm hugged her closer, and he brushed his lips against her forehead. 'You've had a shock,' he murmured. 'You must feel so hurt…'

Frankie's body relaxed and, she confessed to herself won-deringly, she felt a sense of release, of being her own woman. A strange feeling of excitement and danger seemed to flicker through her. She'd been betrayed in the most sudden and shocking way, but it was wonderful to be soothed and comforted, feel the strength of Jack's hard body, his arms wrapped around her.

He smiled down at her. 'This isn't the end of the world. You've made the first step already, putting the past behind you.'

Frankie looked at his eyes, those kind, humorous, eyes and for the first time thought of the word 'sexy' to describe them. She was so close she could see the morning stubble on his chin after a night working in Casualty, feel his breath on her cheek, and it didn't seem at all out of order that he should turn her chin towards him and kiss her lightly on her lips. Suddenly Frankie didn't care whether she was giving Jack the wrong signals. She needed the warmth and affection she'd been missing so much for the past year. She reached up and took off Jack's glasses and pulled his face to hers.

'This makes it easier,' she said softly, and she kissed him full on his lips.

His eyes widened in immediate shocked response, then he sighed and tightened his arms around her, pulling her body to his, his mouth teasing hers open. And it felt so good. Frankie closed her eyes and her back arched against him. She nuzzled his neck and twined her fingers through the hair at the back of his neck. Was it a reaction to the shock she'd just had or was it a symbol of her determination to be free of Damian for ever? It didn't matter, she thought hazily. She was her own woman now and she'd live for the moment.

Jack's kisses became more passionate, his lips tracing a trail down her jawline into the little hollow in her neck, the soft skin of her breast. Frankie leaned into him, revelling in his touch and the electric respónse of every erogenous zone in her body and the almost forgotten feeling of being made love to by a man who was every bit as sexy as Damian had been. She was living for the moment, firmly pushing to the background the blow she'd just had.

He drew back for a second, his blue eyes darkened. 'If we're going to stop perhaps we'd better do so now before it's too late. Are you sure you want this?'

What did she care if they went all the way? She'd just been dumped very publicly and Jack was doing what he could to comfort her. Perhaps it was just a mutual act of release for both of them, two lonely people, but suddenly it seemed a fitting end to one stage of her life and the beginning of another.

Frankie whispered, 'Why not? I'm free now, Jack. I'm not betraying anyone, am I?'

They sank to the floor and Jack looked down at her, supporting himself on his elbows above her. 'Beautiful Francesca,' he whispered. 'You are so desirable—such fire in you.'

His body was heavy on hers but the touch of his kisses were butterfly soft, his hands exploring her most secret places, bringing her to a fever pitch of arousal. And for a while Frankie forgot that she'd just been betrayed by her fiancé and that by rights she should be weeping her eyes out.

Afterwards Jack lifted himself away and lay on the floor beside her, staring for a while up at the ceiling. Frankie propped herself up on one elbow and looked down at him.

'What are you thinking?' she asked.

He smiled and turned his head towards her. 'I was thinking

that it's been a long time since I did that...and it felt good, very good.'

Frankie stared at him rather bleakly. It sounded as if he'd had Sue in his mind as he made love to her, and it was a very peculiar thought. But, then, she'd been under no illusions that Jack still loved his wife, had never got over her. The past half-hour had been therapy for them both—it had just been an episode in their lives.

Jack sat up and reached for his shirt. 'I'll have to go,' he said. 'I've got to drop in on my parents and see Abby. They're looking after her while I'm on night duty. They'll wonder what's happened to me.'

'What will you tell them?'

He grinned. 'That I had to attend an emergency.' He bent over towards her and kissed her softly on her mouth. 'I hope the treatment was helpful?'

A lick of desire flickered again through Frankie's body, a remembrance of their passionate love-making and how wonderful and unexpected it had been. But it all seemed rather like a dream now, hardly real. And the fact that probably Jack had been thinking of Sue as he'd made love to her gave her very mixed feelings. Jack watched her face, then put his thumb under her chin and tipped her face towards him.

'What's the matter?' he said gently. 'Are you regretting what we've just done?'

'Not really regretting it,' she said slowly. 'I'm just thinking that I...well, I rather led you on, didn't I? What was I doing, Jack? Damian and I have only just split up and here I am with someone else!'

A funny little smile flitted across his face. 'What are you

feeling guilty for? You're a free woman now, don't forget. As you said, free to pursue your own life, loves, career.'

Frankie frowned and hugged her arms around herself. 'Is that another way of saying I can be as promiscuous as I like?'

Jack stopped doing up the buttons on his shirt and looked at her with a hint of exasperation. 'For God's sake, Frankie, I know you won't do that.'

'Perhaps I've lost it slightly. Let's face it, no sooner have I finished with one man than I'm in bed with another—an easy lay, in other words.'

He looked at her quizzically, as if he knew that she'd deliberately used words to shock him and convince herself that she was in the wrong. 'I assure you I don't think that of you at all. All I do know is I haven't felt as good as this for a long time.' He squatted down beside her and leaned forward, one arm propped on either side of her. 'I know you don't want any ties…'

Frankie turned away from him and grabbed her clothes, pulling them on quickly, suddenly terrified that she'd done one of the most silly things in her life.

'You're right. I don't want any kind of commitment—and neither do you, of course. This…this was just an episode, a lovely episode, but…'

'Something you'd rather forget, is that it?' His lips gave a little twisted smile. 'I understand what you mean—you've been hurt. As far as sex is concerned, we're just ships that pass in the night—is that it?' He slung his jacket over his shoulders and looked down at her almost wistfully. 'I've helped you achieve what you wanted, though, haven't I?'

She frowned. 'I don't know what you mean.'

'You've managed to obliterate Damian's memory—to get him out of your system.'

'*What?*' Frankie's eyes widened in shocked amazement and she felt her cheeks flame. 'What are you talking about? Are you saying I was using you?'

'Perhaps we were both using each other—isn't that the honest truth? We were trying to comfort each other.'

'But I made all the running, didn't I?' whispered Frankie. 'If I hadn't come on to you like I did, we wouldn't have ended up making love. I came on too strong and gave the wrong messages. You would never have done it or even thought about it if I hadn't—'

'Oh, come on Frankie, stop having this guilt trip,' he said with a grin. 'I'm only human. To say I've never thought of a beautiful girl like you in a sexy way would be a lie. Look, we are two people who needed warmth and affection and we helped each other in that.'

'But it meant no more to you than a comforting cup of cocoa?'

There was something unreadable in those blue eyes. 'A very delicious cup of cocoa,' he said gently. 'But you're a free agent, and I understand that. Wonderful as it was we'll count it as a very happy memory. That's what you want, isn't it?'

Why did she feel so wretched when he said those words? Surely the last thing she needed after Damian's deception was another love affair?

'Yes,' she said in a small voice. Then she flicked a look at Jack's strong, intelligent face and felt a sense of shame. She'd almost forced the man to make love to her. He'd felt an obligation to comfort her, and all the time it had been Sue he'd wanted, and could never have.

'I'm sorry, Jack. Will you forgive me?' she whispered.

'There's nothing to forgive.' His face relaxed into a smile, and he pushed a hand roughly through his hair. 'Hell, Frankie, there was nothing cheap or tawdry about what we did—but let's put it behind us, if that's what you want.'

Frankie stood up and smoothed down her skirt. 'You're right. We'll have to be friends, like we were before.'

She turned her large dark eyes to his and he nodded. 'OK. It's history and we'll forget about it.' He looked at the floor for a moment, arms folded as if he was thinking, then he added, 'When I come to think of it, it's better that way—too many complications happen when sex is involved! I'm Damian's brother-in-law, for one thing. It wouldn't seem right to have an affair with his girlfriend, would it?'

'Ex-girlfriend,' Frankie corrected him with a sigh. 'But you're right. You and Damian shouldn't fall out just because he and I aren't together any more.'

'I doubt we'll be seeing each much in the future,' remarked Jack grimly. He looked at his watch. 'Damn! It's later than I thought. I'll get off to the farm and see Abby before I go home and have a kip.'

'See you tonight at work.' She smiled.

He looked at her rather sadly for a second before he left, and Frankie leant against the door, her thoughts as jumbled as colours in a kaleidoscope. Had she really just made love to Jack Herrick, half an hour after learning that Damian had been two-timing her? And even more extraordinary, while she had been in his arms, it had been the most wonderful, fulfilling experience she'd ever had—it had been as if Damian had never existed at all. But Jack was probably right—she'd just been using him to forget how she'd been betrayed and it could never lead to anything permanent.

She went over to the window and watched Jack get into his car and drive off. It was going to be very difficult to work with him and maintain a friendly detachment. She needed comfort, she needed love, but the last thing she needed was to get entangled in another relationship, wasn't it?

Jack put the car into gear and began the short drive out to his parents' farm. He was going to be later than he'd said, but he'd just made love to Frankie and for a few minutes he'd felt on top of the world. He couldn't believe that it had happened so suddenly, but Frankie had made it very clear that there was to be no repeat of that scenario, that it had really meant nothing to her—and who could blame her? Any girl would be wary of starting a relationship again so soon after being dumped, and she had a great life before her—she could do well in her career now that she could concentrate on it.

He negotiated the twisting drive to the farm. His eyes barely took in where he was driving and he cursed. Making love to Frankie had been wonderful but it had made the future look very, very complicated.

Abby came running out of the farmhouse as he parked and he felt the leap of pride and delight that happened whenever he saw his little girl. She came up to the car window and laughed at him.

'You're late, Daddy! Gran's got breakfast for you before you go and sleep, and it's all dried up and horrid now!'

'I know, sweetheart,' Jack said, getting out of the car and bending down to kiss her. 'I've been very busy at the hospital…'

She took his hand and led him inside, where his mother was sitting at the kitchen table reading the morning paper. Sheila looked up when she saw him come in.

'Well, well, well,' she remarked, getting up and pointing to a photo in the paper. 'I presume you've seen this revelation about Damian. What do you think of it? He seems to have been behaving very badly—at least to Frankie.'

Jack glanced at the paper with the revealing picture of Damian and the film star. 'I did know about it,' he admitted. 'Saw it on a patient's television this morning.'

'Poor Frankie,' exclaimed Sheila. 'That's going to put her off men for ever, I should think.'

'I suppose so,' Jack said hollowly.

'Of course it will,' said his mother indignantly. 'She's been very let down. If she's got any sense she'll keep away from any commitment for a long time. After a shock like that she needs time and space to heal emotionally.' She looked at her son sadly. 'I think I know what I'm talking about, don't you?'

Jack went over to his mother and put his arm round her shoulders. 'Yes, of course you do, Mum,' he said gently. 'When someone betrays you, it can hurt a lot of people. At least when my father left you, eventually Brian came on the scene to pick up the pieces.'

'That's right,' sighed Sheila, looking into the distance. 'How lucky I was—we both were…' Then she gave a little laugh and said briskly, 'Well, we mustn't look back, and neither must Frankie. At least she's got a good job. I had virtually no qualifications. Now, Jack, eat up that congealed food before I give it to the pigs!'

Jack sat down at the table and nodded. Of course his

mother was right. Who had he been kidding when he'd told himself that he and Frankie might get together some day on a permanent basis? It would be grossly unfair of him to assume that eventually they would slip into a commitment—not with the responsibilities that he brought with him. As Frankie had said, she was a free agent now and not about to form ties with anyone. And he himself? Did he not still feel he owed an allegiance to Damian. Wasn't he betraying his oldest friend in some way?

He pushed a piece of bacon listlessly around his plate. One day she would meet someone she could trust again—someone not connected to Damian in any way, and who had no baggage from the past. For his own sake and hers, he had to cool things between them and make sure that the only relationship they had was a working one.

CHAPTER SIX

FRANKIE FROWNED AT the computer screen in front of her as she entered patients' notes, and for the third time that morning pressed the wrong key, sending all the information into some inner file and causing the machine to inform her that she'd performed an illegal action.

'Damn. Not again!'

She leant back in her chair for a second and rubbed her eyes in exasperation, then opened them and gazed in front of her, not seeing the screen but imagining two blue eyes looking into hers intently and a pair of hands moving over her body expertly so that her stomach felt as if a thousand little butterflies were fluttering around in it.

'Oh, God,' she groaned to herself. 'What am I like?'

No matter what she was doing, that picture kept returning, and she was filled with a mixture of guilt and regret that once again her friendship with Jack had been compromised—this time by her. A few weeks ago her engagement to Damian had shattered into a million pieces—and what had she done? Like a fool, she'd immediately leapt into bed with Jack, at least fig-uratively, inevitably changing the dynamics of their relationship. In fact, she reflected wryly, she'd seen very little of Jack since that day. Was he regretting it, too? She wouldn't blame him—and it was all her fault. She had set the pace and now he was probably as embarrassed as she was to be working in the same place. She sighed as she fruitlessly hit more keys on the computer, this time bringing up the words, 'Do you want to rename this file?'

'No, I don't,' she growled irritably.

She swivelled round in her chair and stared down the corridor. All this thinking about Jack was completely wrong. Hadn't she told the man that she wasn't interested in any long-term relationship? She ought to be glad he hadn't contacted her since they'd made love that extraordinary morning—he was only doing what she'd told him to do. She'd been betrayed once very publicly and she should have learnt from that experience that flinging oneself into an affair, like she'd had with Damian, was a recipe for disaster.

Corey slapped some files on the desktop and Frankie jumped out of her reverie. 'Sorry, Frankie, you're wanted in the plaster room of the children's area. A little boy with a broken arm.'

'No problem, Corey. Want to come and do the plaster for me?'

'Sure.' Corey flicked a glance at her friend. 'You OK?'

Frankie smiled to herself. Everyone had been treating her as if she'd been fragile glass when they'd learned about Damian, but there was really little need, she thought almost guiltily. She couldn't confess that almost all her waking thoughts were about another man entirely and she hadn't felt so alive for months!

The plaster room was a bright place with a mural of cartoon characters round the walls, all of whom had bandages or casts on, some waving crutches, others taking medicine. The staff had given their own time to paint it and it was a marvellous distraction for frightened children to look at. The little boy sitting on the edge of the bed, however, had scared eyes behind owlish wire glasses perched on the end of his freckled nose and a quiff of red hair standing up on his forehead. He looked mournfully at Frankie, and a big tear rolled down his cheek, which he hastily brushed away with his sleeve. Sitting at the side of the room was the woman who'd brought him in, a thin, nervous person with nicotine stained fingers holding another small child on her knee.

'You'll be fine, Jimmy,' Frankie said kindly. 'How old are you pet?'

'Six.'

'And how did you break your arm?'

'Fooling around,' broke in the woman. 'I told him to keep quiet and watch television, but what does he do? He only jumps down the kitchen steps onto a plant pot, that's what!'

The child looked nervously at the woman, then whispered, 'It wasn't just me. Barney was helping me…'

'But it was you that managed to fall, wasn't it? I told you to keep inside and not make a noise while I was out—little brat.'

The woman's voice was rough and slightly slurred and she had an unkempt look about her. Frankie looked at her sharply and then at Jimmy, his little figure sitting with a slumped back on the table. He looked very miserable, trying not to cry and using the knuckles of one grubby hand to rub his eyes. Frankie put a gentle arm on his shoulder and looked at his arm.

'You know, Jimmy, when we put the cast on this arm, it's going to feel so much better. Look! You see that little dip?

That's where the crack is in your bone. But, I promise you, it won't take all that long to heal. I'll show you the photograph we took of it.'

Frankie passed the woman to hook the X-ray of the child's arm over the viewing light, and she caught the stale smell of smoke and alcohol.

'Are you Jimmy's mother?' she enquired as she looked at the X-ray.

'No. I'm the holiday childminder—got three of them to look after.'

'So where's the third child?' asked Frankie. 'Who's looking after him?'

'I left him with a neighbour—he's all right.'

Alarm bells rang in Frankie's mind. She turned round and looked at the woman. 'You're a registered childminder?'

The woman shifted nervously in her seat. 'I look after me friend's children, if that's what you mean. She doesn't pay me much.'

'And your name is?'

'Mrs Coombs.'

Frankie nodded. She would deal with her concerns about the woman later. Now she needed to look after Jimmy.

'Look, Jimmy,' she said brightly, 'that's a photo of your arm—you can see where you hurt it. You've broken your radius bone. Lots of little boys and girls do that when they have accidents—and they all get better very quickly!'

She went back to the little boy and sat on the chair by him. 'If you look at both arms, you'll see the difference between the good one and the one you've hurt.'

The child looked down at his thin little arms and Frankie

pointed to the concave 'dish' of the fracture. She frowned suddenly, and bent over both limbs as if examining something, then transferred her attention to his legs. She straightened up without comment and grinned reassuringly at Jimmy.

'Now Nurse Corey's going to put a cast on your arm—it won't hurt because she's so good at doing it.'

Corey was preparing glass-fibre bandaging. She looked across at Jimmy and winked at him. 'It won't take a minute to put this on and then when it's hard you can get all the other children in the class to sign it and draw pictures on it—it'll look cool!'

Jimmy's sad eyes looked a little brighter. 'Someone in our class had a cast on her leg last term—we all drew on it as well!'

'There you are, then.' Frankie stroked his head. 'Now you've got to help Nurse, Jimmy. Hold your arm still while she winds the bandage round, so when it gets dry it will be really hard and protect your arm.'

The child's elbow was supported on a padded block of wood and Corey wound the bandage evenly round the sleeve that was over his arm, taking care that no creases formed. After she'd finished, she leant back.

'There, young man—a work of art, that is! What about a sticker for Jimmy, Dr Lovatt? He's been a very brave boy.'

Frankie showed Jimmy the sticker that read, 'Gold Star Patient—For Being Very Brave', and then pressed it on his T-shirt.

'Well done, Jimmy,' she said, smiling down at the little boy who smiled shyly back, a faint flush of pink on his cheeks. 'Not many people get those!'

'Perhaps you'll behave yourself now and do what you're told!' said Mrs Coombs sharply from the corner.

Jimmy flinched as if he'd been struck, then his eyes flickered away from her, the smile disappearing from his face and a blank expression replacing it.

'We need Jimmy to stay here for a few minutes while we make sure this sets properly.' Frankie's voice was smooth but firm. 'I should like you to wait in the waiting room with the other little one. Jimmy won't be long. By the way have you let his mother know about his accident?'

'Not yet—there wasn't time,' said the woman sullenly.

'I presume you've given Jimmy's home address and next of kin particulars in at the desk—have they got his mother's work number?'

Mrs Coombs nodded. 'I was going to ring her meself.'

Mrs Coombs and the other child went out. Frankie grimaced and walked across to Corey saying in a quiet voice, 'Mrs Coombs wasn't too impressive, was she? I'm pretty sure that the woman isn't a registered childminder, and the authorities should know she's drinking—and the mother should know that, too.'

'Sounds as if she left the kids alone as well. Who will you inform?'

'Well Jack is the infirmary's representative on the Denniston Child Abuse Committee—I'd better get him involved.' Frankie's stomach did a quick revolution as she anticipated seeing him again. 'I'll find out where he is and put him in the picture. Stay with Jimmy for a minute—I'd like Jack to have a closer look at those marks on his arms and legs…'

She walked briskly down the corridor, her heart rate accelerating when she saw Jack talking to Sister Kenney at the desk. He was wearing the usual hospital greens—a tunic and trousers, the short-sleeved tunic open at the neck. He looked like someone auditioning for the post of a doctor in a medical soap—tall, with a good physique and a humorous intelligent face. He made Damian look brash and overbearing, Frankie thought suddenly. Jack had style, but in a restrained and discreet way.

He looked up from the files he was examining with Sister Kenney as Frankie approached and their eyes met in a flicker of attraction, so quickly that perhaps she imagined it, for a moment later his expression was serious, his tone professional.

'Need any help?' he asked briskly.

'We've just seen a little boy with a greenstick fracture, but Corey and I believe the childminder who brought him in may be drinking heavily. And I have a few question marks about the bruises and some other marks I've seen on his limbs.'

'You think they could be non-accidental injuries?'

She nodded. 'I know we can't leap to conclusions.'

'I'll come and look at him,' Jack said, putting down the files on the desk. 'We'll try and bring in his mother—we need to talk to her. I'll buzz the social worker and she can get onto it.'

They started walking down the corridor and Frankie said, 'There's also the possibility she left this young patient and another child unsupervised. I think you ought to interview her.'

'Don't worry, I'll certainly do that—and I'll draft a report for the social services. I'll talk to them before we inform the police.'

At the door Jack held her elbow to stop her going through for a second and looked down at her, his voice crisp and businesslike. 'How are you—coping all right?'

'Sure I am,' Frankie said brightly. She paused for a second, then spoke in a rush. 'Things happened rather fast the other day—I…I was a fool.'

A little smile flickered at the corner of his mouth. 'Don't worry about it—I've forgotten about it already.' He paused for a second and added, 'I just wondered if you'd heard any more from Damian.'

Frankie looked uncomfortable, embarrassed that he should dismiss their love-making so easily—it made it seem as casual as shaking hands—but perhaps it was better to keep quiet on that.

She shrugged. 'Frankly, I don't want to see or hear from him again.'

Jack nodded. 'I hope you don't. At least now you know now why he left you—although it was cruel not to tell you to your face.'

'To be honest, I don't feel anything for him now,' remarked Frankie as they went into the plaster room.

And that was true, Frankie thought to herself in surprise. A short time ago she had been sure she'd been completely in love with Damian—but that love seemed to have melted like snow in the sun and to be part of a past world. Now…well. She flicked a glance at Jack and felt a shiver of attraction flash through her body. Surely, she wasn't setting off down another road of no return? Jack still mourned his lovely Sue— he'd practically said so, and he wasn't ready to commit to anyone yet.

Corey was reading to Jimmy from one of the story books that were kept in a cupboard and Frankie pushed all thoughts of Jack out of her head and concentrated on the little boy with the mournful face.

'Now, Jimmy,' said Frankie, 'this is Dr Herrick—he wants

to see what a good job Nurse Corey has made of that cast on your arm.'

Jack squatted down beside the little boy and made a great play of inspecting the cast. 'Hello Jimmy. My goodness, that's an excellent cast—is it comfortable?'

The child nodded and Jack took the opportunity to look closely at the marks on the child's legs and arms. He took a pen from his pocket and drew a funny picture of a cat with a bandaged leg on the cast and wrote, 'To Jimmy from the doctors and nurses at the Infirmary.'

'There you are mate—that proves it's authentic!'

Jimmy gave Jack the first real smile they'd seen all morning and he looked proudly down at his arm. 'That's great!' he said.

Jack's bleeper went and he lifted the phone on the wall to see who wanted him. After a few seconds of conversation he turned round and smiled at Jimmy.

'Your mum's on her way up—she wants to see what you've done to yourself.'

A few seconds later a young woman with Jimmy's red hair and large eyes was ushered into the room. She couldn't have been more than twenty-one. She went over to Jimmy and gave him a hug and he wound his arms tightly round her, tears spilling out of his eyes.

'Oh, Jimmy, love, your poor little kid. What've you done to yourself?' She turned round to the staff watching her. 'I came as quick as I could. I didn't have the money for a taxi, so I had to get the bus. Where's Mrs Coombs?' She looked puzzled. 'Did she bring Jimmy in?'

'She's in the reception area at the moment. She's your

childminder, isn't she?' Jack's voice was gentle—he didn't want to antagonise the girl.

'Yeah, she looks after the three of them while I'm at work. She lives next door, so it's easy for me to drop them off.'

'Has she always looked after children?'

'Yes—she has quite a few children some days, but she doesn't charge all that much, so it makes it worth my while to work.'

'OK. It's Ms Bayliss, isn't it? I wonder if you could spare a moment to talk to me in the office—this room will probably be needed soon.'

Ms Bayliss looked wary. 'Is something wrong?'

'We just need a few details. If Jimmy comes, too, he can bring that book with him while we talk.' Jack smiled reassuringly at the young woman. 'It won't take long. I'll be with you in a minute. Corey, can you take Jimmy and his mum?'

The mother and child went out and Frankie said, 'What do you think? Those weren't just bruises on Jimmy's legs, were they?'

Jack shook his head grimly. 'They look very like burn marks—cigarette burns. I've seen those marks before on other children, and the signs unfortunately all point to child abuse. I'll go and talk to the mother and try and find out more about Mrs Coombs. The social worker's coming down, too.'

'Poor little Jimmy…at the mercy of a woman like that.'

'There's too many little Jimmys out there.' Jack sighed. 'I can't say I'm very fond of this aspect of the job, but if it helps the Jimmys of this world it's worth doing.' He started to go out of the door and nodded at her. 'I'll write a report on this one and send you a copy.'

His voice was brisk, neither friendly nor unfriendly and

Frankie went back to the computer with the distinct impression that he had put what had happened between them firmly in the past. She tried to ignore the funny little hollow feeling in her heart that there seemed to be nothing between them at all now. She should have been relieved, but for some reason she felt quite depressed.

'Darling! You look lovely—that colour suits you so well, and I love your hair up like that!'

'Cost a fortune.' Frankie grinned. 'But I couldn't let the side down could I on a night like this.'

Mrs Lovatt smiled in pride at Frankie. She gave her daughter a light kiss and held her hands looking into her face searchingly. 'Are you all right, Frankie, after that ghastly man let you down?'

Frankie had finally told her parents, and they had been their usual supportive selves, telling her that she was far too good for him and that in no time she'd find someone new.

'I'm fine, Mum. I should have realised the truth about him ages ago. I'm better off without him.'

And she meant it, thought Frankie. She'd been clinging to an illusion and in a way it had been almost a relief to find out the truth about Damian.

'I'm so glad. We've been worried about you—but now I see how gorgeous you look I realise it's done you no harm at all! Come into the small hall and have a drink. Let me introduce you to everybody.'

Mrs Lovatt led the way into the oak-panelled room that was off the University Great Hall. There were paintings of previous university dignitaries round the walls, and it looked out onto a beautiful courtyard with Virginia creeper over the mellow brick building, the late sun making the room look warm and glowing. A number of people were murmuring in conversation and sipping the champagne cocktails that Professor Lovatt liked to offer his guests. Frankie knew quite a few of his colleagues and friends.

'We asked the head of the medical faculty to bring along a friend or two from the hospital,' whispered her mother. 'We thought it would make for an easier evening for you if you knew some of the guests. I was pleased to see that you've worked closely with one of them.'

'Who is it?' asked Frankie with interest.

Her mother nodded over to the other side of the room. 'It's Jack Herrick,' she said. 'I know he's Damian's friend, but I've always thought what a pleasant man he is, and at least you have something in common as you work together!'

Frankie closed her eyes for a second as if to obliterate the sight of Jack looking fabulous in a dinner suit, talking to someone in the corner. How was she going pass a few hours with Jack in polite conversation when they'd agreed to keep apart, and he was making it very clear that he wanted it that way? She opened her eyes to find her mother looking at her anxiously.

'Is that all right, darling—not awkward at all?'

What could she say? 'Of course not, Mum. We'll have a lovely time!'

Frankie swallowed a large mouthful of champagne cocktail, hoping she'd be able to act naturally for the evening with Jack. At the moment he was in intimate conversation with a petite blonde woman, who was laughing immoderately at what he was saying, her hand on his arm in a proprietorial way.

Frankie drained her glass and her mother introduced her to one of her father's colleagues who had come for the ceremony. His name was Gordon Hubner, a stocky American with a pleasant face and an enthusiastic manner. He was amusing and flattering, obviously very taken by Professor Lovatt's daughter.

Across the room, Jack watched her covertly as he sipped his champagne and listened to the blonde woman chattering by his side. Frankie's dress was cut low, its warm peach colour giving her skin a golden glow and showing off the soft swell of her breasts. She was slim but the dress's nipped-in waist made her slender figure look voluptuous. He sighed. How could he ever have thought that he and she could be an item? She could have her pick of any of the eligible men around. It just wouldn't be fair to clip her wings with the responsibilities that he had, to assume that she would want to take on the mantle of mother to a five-year-old child. He turned back politely to listen to what the blonde woman was saying to him.

'Time to make our way through to the Grand Hall now, everybody,' called out Mrs Lovatt after a short time, clapping her hands for attention. 'You'll find names on the seats so that you'll know where to sit.'

Gordon Hubner shepherded Frankie, his hand on her arm, to the enormous hall where all the important occasions took place.

'Dammit, we're not sitting together,' he said. 'I'll see you later when we have dinner. I'll save you a seat.'

In the Great Hall Frankie found herself beside Jack, with the blonde woman she had seen him talking to earlier sitting on his other side. He smiled politely at her as they prepared to sit.

'I didn't realise we were in the same party,' he remarked.

'No, I didn't either—that is, I didn't know you'd be here,' she replied, her words rather jumbled out of stiff lips.

He turned to the girl on his other side and introduced them. 'This is a colleague of mine—Francesca Lovatt, Professor Lovatt's daughter. And this is Penny Curtis, who lectures in history here.'

Both women nodded to each other and Jack started looking at his programme while Penny talked to a man on her other side. An unnatural silence seemed to hang between Frankie and Jack, although they were so close together. Nearly as close, thought Frankie wryly, as they had been when they'd been making love on the carpet in her house. She flicked a glance at his strong hands leafing through the programme, a few dark hairs showing under the cuffs of his shirtsleeves. Those hands had brought her to a pitch of excitement not long ago, and an image of the two of them locked in the most intimate of embraces seemed to loom up before her. She bit her lip. It was going to be a hard few hours. Jack obviously didn't want to talk and she…she was gradually beginning to realise that what she really longed for was to feel his body even closer to hers and his lips kissing her with those soft butterfly kisses that he'd showered on her the other day.

To Frankie's relief, the ceremony started very quickly. Honorary degrees were given out and then finally her father was installed as the Vice Chancellor. Mrs Lovatt looked across at her daughter and there were tears of pride in their eyes, Frankie thinking what an amazing climb her father had had up the ladder of success, from the son of a miner to a university professor when no one in his family before him had attended school beyond the age of fifteen.

As if reading her thoughts, Jack turned to her and said politely, 'What a wonderful climax to your father's career—you must be delighted.'

'I am—we're so proud of him. He's made his own way in the world from a deprived background, but he's very focussed. When he sets his heart on something he usually achieves it—but that doesn't mean he's ruthless,' she added quickly.

'Ah,' said Jack, looking at her with a little smile. 'It's not wrong to be ambitious though—your career means a lot to you now, doesn't it?'

Frankie nodded. 'If you mean since my break-up with Damian, yes, I feel I've got a lot to give—and a lot to learn, of course.'

People began to move from their seats and make their way to the huge refectory which had been turned into a ballroom for the evening and decorated with streamers and balloons and drifts of glittering silver paper from the ceiling. Professor Lovatt's party was sitting at a large table set for the meal, with an exotic arrangement of flowers in the middle. Frankie sat down next to her father and Gordon, who had commandeered two seats before any one else could get them. Jack sat opposite Frankie next to Penny.

It was a pleasant evening. Frankie chattered brightly to everyone, determined that no one should think she was still upset by her broken engagement. Occasionally Jack would flick a glance at her animated face, a faint flush of colour on her cheeks and her glossy chestnut hair like a halo round her head. Just as they were finishing their meal there was a loud 'twang' and a very much amplified electric guitar crashed into a chord that made most of the room jump before a group on stage flung themselves into a raucous first number.

Frankie looked up at the stage where they were playing and started to laugh. Hurling himself into the throes of an energetic routine while playing the guitar was a familiar figure—or at least someone she'd met before. She looked across at Jack and his eyes met hers with a glimmer of humour in their depths.

'Seems Denver Clayton's made a good recovery,' he commented. 'Let's hope he's not off for a Chinese meal later!'

Penny leaned forward and said with interest. 'Do you know this group then?'

'This is the first time I've heard them,' said Jack. 'But I have met him before.' He declined to say where or when that had happened.

'They're great, aren't they? I love dancing to them,' said Penny pointedly, pushing back her thick blonde hair from her forehead and smiling widely at Jack.

He took the hint. 'Do you want to give it a try?' He smiled.

Frankie watched them as they circled the floor—the music was quite fast and furious and Jack whirled Penny round, catching her when she spun one way and then the other. He made it seem effortless, his tall figure moving rhythmically to the music, long legs agile—for a serious-looking man he looked as if he enjoyed dancing.

I've never danced with him, Frankie said to herself wistfully. And I probably never will now.

The evening drew to a close. Frankie had danced with Gordon for most of the time, interspersed with friends from other tables. She and Jack did not dance together, but she'd enjoyed herself, she thought defiantly, shown that she could have a good evening without having a special man by her side. She went to the Ladies for a minute to renew her make-up and when she returned to the table, Jack was sitting by himself. Gordon was now dancing with Penny.

Frankie sat primly and rather self-consciously near Jack, hoping that her parents would come back to the table to lighten the atmosphere. After a few seconds of silence he glanced across at her and said evenly. 'Perhaps we ought to have a dance—it looks rather odd that we're the only people not on the floor.'

'Do you think so?' Frankie's heart began to thump rather quickly.

Their eyes clashed, wary, watchful, then Jack leant over and refilled her glass of wine and his own and took a long drink before saying slowly, 'I wondered if it might not be in the rules of engagement. We did, after all, say we didn't want to get too, er…close,' he murmured.

'I know,' she said in a small voice. 'You're right—after what happened, do you think it would be wise?'

Jack stood up and took her hand, pulling her up beside him. 'It probably isn't wise,' he remarked lightly. 'But it's the last dance.'

How could she refuse? Hadn't it been what she'd been longing to do most of the evening? He led her onto the dance floor, and the lights dimmed for the end of the evening, anonymous figures swirling past them in the gloom. And as soon as she felt his body close to hers, Frankie realised that it wasn't wise—not very wise at all.

CHAPTER SEVEN

THE MUSIC WAS slow and languorous, and Jack put his arms around Frankie, drawing her so close to him that she could feel his body pressed against hers, the movement of his thighs in rhythm with her legs. Her heart thumped uncomfortably against her chest. This was like some kind of heavenly torture to her, feeling his breath on her cheek, smelling the male smell of him and realising that what she'd once felt for Damian was as nothing compared to what she was now beginning to feel for Jack.

Eventually he spoke. 'I didn't mean to dance with you tonight, Frankie,' he said quietly. 'I told myself it would do neither of us any good at all. You don't want a relationship, and I...well, I don't think it would be right for me to get involved either.'

'Then why *are* you dancing with me?' She looked up at him rather impudently, her eyes wide and innocent.

He looked at her gravely. 'I told you—because it looks bad if we're the only people left in the room that aren't dancing.'

He didn't add, 'And because you look so sexy in this dress,' but he slid his hand up behind her head and pressed it against his chest so that she could feel the reverberation of his heart.

Frankie gave herself up to the dreamy, relaxed atmosphere of the room, a dizzy happiness flickering through her, a feeling that whatever they did tonight, she didn't care!

He looked down at her. 'Are you enjoying this?' he said softly.

'Of course I am.'

'It's not in line with what we agreed—you told me we should keep a distance from each other.'

'I know I did.' She looked up at him and whispered, 'You're holding me much too closely, by the way.'

He gave a low laugh. 'I'm trying not to get too intimate, but I could hold you much closer, actually—shall I show you what I mean?'

'No…no…'

Her voice faded as he tightened his arms around her body and in the darkness of the room put his mouth down to hers and brushed her lips with his, turning her bones to jelly.

'We shouldn't be doing this,' she whispered. 'What will my parents and everyone else think?'

'We're not doing anything wrong,' Jack said. 'And I've been thinking about the other day…you were living for the moment then, two people just enjoying sex for it's own sake. Isn't that right?'

Put like that, it sounded rather impersonal, thought Frankie wryly. 'I told you,' she protested. 'It was wonderful—and it wasn't "just enjoying sex", as you put it…'

'I'll put it another way, then. Let's enjoy tonight, and think of it for what it is—an evening for fun between friends with no commitments. And I assure you it won't go any further than this…'

His mouth was on hers again, but this time he teased her

lips apart, making her insides liquefy with a tantalising longing. Surely this wasn't the way mere friends behaved? Frankie leant into his chest and revelled in the melding of their bodies as they matched the rhythm of the music. Why, she wondered desperately, had she declared that she didn't want a relationship with any man after Damian? She was beginning to realise that a future with Jack was something that seemed more and more attractive—only he didn't want commitment, did he? He hadn't said it outright, but she was certain that he was implying that in his heart he was still committed to his wife.

Gradually the music came to a halt, the lights went up. She was still swaying with the rhythm, her eyes closed, when Jack stepped back and gazed quizzically down at her.

'Thank you for a very pleasant dance,' he said formally. He put his hand out and brushed a tendril of hair from her face. 'A nice little interlude?'

'Exactly,' she agreed lightly, smiling at him and trying very hard to disguise what had suddenly struck her like a thunderbolt in the past few minutes—she had fallen for Jack, hook, line and sinker! The 'nice little interlude' for him had been rather a momentous eye-opener for her. She wanted to spend every night pressed to that muscular body, feeling the thump of his heart against her, drowning in the look of his eyes…

She turned and walked briskly back to the table, turning her head to smile at people she knew, trying to convey the impression that the dance had been nothing more than a social exchange.

Jack waited for a moment, watching Frankie as she greeted

everyone else at the table. I shouldn't have danced with her, he thought gloomily. It had been a stupid thing to do. Feeling her in his arms again had just been twisting the knife when he knew there was no future between them—she'd made that very clear.

As Jack pulled back a chair for Frankie, a ringing tone came from his jacket and with a sigh he reached into his pocket and pulled out his mobile phone.

'Who the hell can be calling at this time of night?' He frowned. 'I hope it's not my mother to say Abby's not well or something…' He put the phone to his ear and listened, his expression changing.

'What is it?' asked Frankie when he'd finished talking to the caller. 'Is it about Abby?'

He shook his head. 'It's not Abby,' he said. 'It's my mother. Something seems to be the matter with her leg—she's in great pain, but she refuses to let my father send for an ambulance.'

'Has she fallen?'

'I don't know, but I'll have to go. Will you make my apologies to your mother and father? I'm really sorry…'

'I'm coming with you,' declared Frankie. 'Perhaps I can be of some help—look after Abby if you have to take your mother to hospital.'

He hesitated for a second, then nodded. 'Thanks, that's a good idea. My father did sound distraught, and he's not one to flap so I guess it's serious. Although if either of them were ill, I'd have thought it would have been Brian. My mother's always been the physically stronger, and she hardly ever gives in to illness.'

* * *

The lights in the farmhouse were on when they drove up and Brian was waiting in the porch, leaning on his stick, the anxious look on his face replaced by one of relief when he saw his son.

'I'm so sorry to drag you away, but I don't know what to do about Sheila. Her leg looks terrible—absolutely huge and red. She banged it earlier today on a corner of the coffee-table just as we were off to see a friend of hers. By the time we came home it was beginning to get more and more painful.'

'Well, let's go and look at it,' said Jack briskly.

They went into the sitting room where Sheila was lying on the couch, her leg propped up on a cushion.

'Brian shouldn't have brought you back from the dance,' she said crossly. 'He's such a fusspot. I told him that by tomorrow it would have gone down, but he won't take any notice of me.'

Jack sat down beside her and pushed up her skirt so that both legs could be seen. One of the legs looked elephantine beside the other, mottled red and blue. Jack felt the leg gently and Sheila gave a sharp intake of breath and winced.

'This looks pretty horrible,' observed Jack. 'I think Dad did the right thing to get me and I'm going to give you the same advice. You need to get to hospital.'

'But surely if it's an infection, you can give me antibiotics.'

'We don't know what's causing it yet.' Jack grinned down at her. 'Trust me, mum, I'm a doctor. And I'm sure Frankie agrees with me.'

Frankie nodded. 'It might not be an infection. It could be a DVT—deep vein thrombosis.'

'Well, give me an aspirin or something—doesn't that thin the blood?'

Brian banged on the floor with his stick. 'For goodness' sake, woman, do as they say! I can deal with everything here…you're as stubborn as a mule!'

Sheila looked angrily at the circle of people round her. 'This is quite ridiculous. Going into hospital for a sore leg. Brian can't do without me on the farm because I sort out the paperwork, and there's Abby…'

Jack held up his hand. 'Stop, Mum! Until tests have been done, no one can say for sure what's wrong with this leg.' Then he took her hand and held it gently in his, realising that her bluster was because, like so many people who were rarely ill, she was frightened. 'The sooner they deal with this, the sooner you'll be home.'

'And I'll stay with Abby,' said Frankie quickly. 'I'll be glad to. And surely the paperwork can wait for a day or two?'

Sheila subsided back against the sofa and sighed. 'I can tell you won't rest until you've got me into hospital,' she said with a wan smile, but behind the show of reluctance there was relief in her eyes. 'And what kind of tests do they do anyway?'

'Nothing that hurts. Probably Doppler ultrasound scanning, or they may introduce a dye into the vein and take an X-ray—that will show up a thrombosis if there is one.'

'I just hope they know what they're doing,' Sheila said darkly.

Jack's eyes twinkled. 'I should hope they do. Denniston A and E is where Frankie and I both work, remember—any blunders and they'll have us to answer to! They'll get a shock when they see me coming in dressed in a dinner jacket tonight!'

The ambulance wasn't long in coming, giving Frankie

enough time to pack a few things for Sheila to take in with her and to reassure her that Abby would be fine.

'I'll stay here tonight and tomorrow if need be,' she said. 'I'm not in on duty until Monday—and you may be back by then. If not, I believe you have a help that comes in anyway.'

'I'm so grateful to you,' said Sheila. 'I know Abby will be thrilled that you're here to look after her.'

'I'll bring Dad back here,' said Jack. 'I'm pretty sure you'll be kept in for a day or two, but I have the day off tomorrow as well, so between us things will run as smoothly as clockwork!'

When the ambulance came, Brian went in it with Sheila. Jack was going to follow in the car. He turned to Frankie for a second as he went out of the door.

'You're a star,' he said simply. He ran his hand distractedly through his hair and sighed. 'This is one of the many times when I miss having Sue around to help.'

As Frankie lay in the Herricks' spare bed, listening to the unfamiliar creaks and sounds in the old farmhouse, Jack's words echoed in her mind. No woman was going to measure up to his dead wife, she thought sadly. Sue was still a presence in his life even now. Frankie tossed restlessly under the sheet. This evening she'd confronted the truth—that it wasn't just lust she felt for Jack. She loved him—and it was going to be an uphill climb to persuade him to love her as well!

The sun made a warm pool of light on the bed, waking Frankie up and making her wonder for a second where on earth she was. There was a scrabbling at the bedroom door and a little giggle, and Frankie lifted her head from the pillow and looked curiously at the door as it opened and a large dog bounded into the room, followed closely by Abby's little figure, carefully carrying a small tray with a glass of milk on it.

'Brindle and I thought we'd come and wake you up,' announced Abby. She put the tray carefully on the floor and scrambled up onto the bed. 'Daddy thought you might like some milk. I didn't know you were staying with us—I was very surprised!'

'I hope you were pleased as well,' said Frankie amused by the grave way Abby spoke. 'And how kind of you to bring me milk—just what I feel like!'

'Will you get up now?' asked the little girl. 'I want to show you the farm.'

'I wonder how your granny is?' asked Frankie, sitting up and sipping the cold milk.

'She's all right. They've found something in her leg, but I don't know what it is.'

'I'll come down when I've dressed and find out,' declared Frankie. 'Perhaps you could stop Brindle worrying my shoes, then I can wear them!' she added, watching the dog playing with her best high-heeled shoes, which she'd worn at the dance the night before.

'And what,' she said to herself, 'am I going to wear today—the evening dress I had on last night?'

It seemed the only thing to do. She didn't like to go looking through Sheila's things to find something suitable. When she went down to the kitchen dressed in the peach-coloured dress, Abby gave a whoop of delight.

'You look like a fairy godmother,' she cried. 'Really, really beautiful!'

I look like an idiot, thought Frankie wryly as she caught a

glimpse of herself in the large kitchen mirror. She hunted for an apron—no way dared she spatter fat on this dress, which had cost a fortune!

Nobody else seemed to be about. From what Abby said, Frankie assumed Jack and Brian were both back in the house, though she doubted whether they were still asleep. She looked around the sunny kitchen. It was a true farmhouse kitchen, with an Aga against one wall and a huge wooden table in the middle of the room. There were dried flowers hanging in bunches over an archway that led through to a family room and ceramic pots filled with herbs on a shelf over the Aga. Out of the window she could see the cobbled courtyard surround by the barn and cowshed—it had an old-world look that was charming and disguised the hard work that kept the whole place looking neat and well cared-for. It was an idyllic place for a family and Frankie could imagine the young Jack whirling around the yard on his bike and running over the fields she could see in the distance.

'Shall I make us all a nice big breakfast, Abby?' she said. 'Bacon and eggs—and some cereal first, if you like? You'll have to show me where everything is.'

Abby scampered happily around the kitchen, finding everything she thought Frankie would want, putting cutlery on the table and milk into a big blue striped jug, chattering happily as she did so.

'Daddy says he's tired because he was dancing last night.' She giggled. 'And he said all the girls trod on his toes!'

'Did he indeed?' said Frankie with amusement. 'Where are your daddy and your grandfather?' she asked as she put some bacon under the grill.

'Oh, Grandpa's milking the cows,' said Abby. 'He'll nearly be finished now, and Daddy's having a shower—he'll be ages.'

'No, he won't, young lady,' said Jack's voice from the door. 'It's only taken me five minutes.'

He came into the kitchen and regarded Frankie with raised brows. 'I like the formal look,' he murmured.

Frankie grinned. 'I do feel a little overdressed.'

'You look like a beautiful princess,' Abby informed her. 'I'm going to get the dog now—he's gone into the yard and he's not supposed to when the cows are being milked.'

She ran out and Jack smiled. 'She's absolutely right—you do look like a beautiful princess.'

'Don't be daft. I'll go home after breakfast and put on some sensible clothes. Tell me how Sheila is.'

'It was chaos last night in A and E, and she won't have her scan till this morning, but it's almost certainly a thrombosis,' Jack said. 'She's seeing Mr Curtis, the vascular consultant, later today, but at the moment she's on anti-coagulents. I think that will do the trick—but if we hadn't come I doubt if Dad could have persuaded her to go to hospital. She likes to feel she's invincible.'

Frankie laughed. 'Some people pester doctors when there's nothing the matter with them, and others won't come near a medic even if they're seriously ill!'

They looked at each other in mutual amusement, Jack's blue eyes holding hers. A crackle of excitement flickered through her. She turned away hastily and began breaking the eggs into the frying-pan. He came over to the stove and leant against the wall, watching her cooking.

'I hoped you enjoyed last night,' he said. 'It was a good do, wasn't it—before we had to leave?'

Enjoyed it? Francesca sighed. He'd no idea how much she'd enjoyed it, revelled in it, hadn't stopped thinking about it. She'd thought it would never happen again, the two of them close to each other—as close as two people could possibly be without actually being in bed together... Had it only been last night that she'd realised that the attraction she felt for him wasn't just lust? What had started as attraction had turned to love in the time it took to do one dance. She hadn't been prepared for it to hit her like this.

'I thought it was a...a very nice evening,' she replied, slipping the eggs and bacon deftly onto a plate. 'And now get this down you and I'll go and find your daughter and Brian and tell them breakfast is ready.'

Jack sat down at the table. 'You know,' he said casually, 'Abby and I are going for a picnic this afternoon at the beach—you wouldn't think of coming, too, would you?'

'Would you not want to see your mother? I can look after Abby.'

'I'll pop in quickly this morning, but I guess Dad will want to be with her most of the time. And I did promise Abby we'd give the dog a good run on the beach—and even go a short swim in the sea if it's warm enough.'

Frankie shuddered. 'Surely it'll be freezing? I'd enjoy a walk on the beach, but count me out of a swim.'

Jack waved his fork towards the window. 'It's going to be a lovely day—pack your bikini anyway.'

Outside she could see Abby playing with the dog, tugging a piece of rope that he was worrying. It would be fun to do something in the afternoon with the little girl, instead of going back home and sitting by herself. And, of course, Jack would be there as well…

'I'll go home and get into more suitable gear.' She smiled. 'And I'll bring the food.'

'Then I'll pick you up early this afternoon.'

It was a sparkling afternoon, the sea glinting in the warm sunshine and the sands a golden ribbon along the water's edge. Definitely not warm enough for a swim, thought Frankie firmly, although there were quite a few children splashing around in the shallows. Some way down the beach a small flotilla of sand yachts were skimming across the sand, their bright sails like so many large butterflies.

As soon as the dog saw the beach he bounded along joyously until he came to the sea and then splashed in and out of the waves.

'Brindle doesn't mind the water,' said Jack.

'It doesn't mean it's warm enough for humans,' declared Frankie.

Jack grinned at her. 'It'll do your circulation good.'

'Stop it completely, you mean!'

They put their rugs and chairs down in front of the sand dunes and within sight of a vigorous game of cricket being played by a group of children with an enthusiastic man organising them. Abby wandered over and looked wistfully at them. She was much younger than the other children, but it didn't stop her walking to the edge of the game and longing to be part of it.

'Poor Abby,' remarked Jack as he sat down. 'She loves to be included in everything—it's hard, being an only child.'

'Like both of us,' observed Frankie, putting up a little

folding table and placing the basket full of food and drink on top of it. 'Did you ever miss having siblings?'

'I've always wanted to be part of a large family—and you?'

'Of course. It would have taken the pressure off my parents' ambitions for me, I suppose.'

'I know what you mean—and Abby is always saying how much she'd like a brother or sister.'

'I'm sure it'll happen someday.'

Jack laughed. 'You can't do these things to order, you know. Not many women would want to take on the responsibility of someone else's child.'

Frankie wanted to shout, 'I do! She's a lovely little girl and we'd get along fine!' Instead, she said quietly, 'I'm sure loads of women would love to look after a child like Abby…'

Jack flicked a glance at her, then watched a handful of sand slip through his fingers. 'Being a step-parent isn't easy,' he said after a pause.

'How do you know? That can't always be the case,' protested Frankie. She undid a flask and started to pour some tea into the mugs she'd bought.

'Of course it's not always so,' he conceded, accepting a mug of the hot liquid and sipping it. 'It so happens I've had firsthand experience of it, though.'

'But surely Brian and Sheila…?'

'Brian is my stepfather, and although I was only seven when my mother and he married, it wasn't an easy relationship between Brian and me at first.'

'I never realised… Were your parents divorced?'

Jack nodded. 'My father left my mother for someone at work and went to live abroad. I never saw him again and I

resented Brian taking his place. Of course now I'm very fond
of him—he's been a great father to me—but I guess I gave
him a hell of a time when he first came to the house!' He gave
a short laugh. 'I wouldn't want to put a new wife through that
sort of thing!'

'But Abby's younger than you were—she probably doesn't
remember Sue all that well,' pointed out Frankie.

'No,' Jack agreed sadly. 'She won't remember her mother
now—not really.'

There was a silence between them. They both watched
Abby's little figure running energetically for a ball—she'd evidently joined in the cricket match and was enjoying it,
judging from the sound of her laughter. She turned round and
called to her father.

'Come on, Daddy, Frankie—they want you to do some
fielding. They need more people!'

Jack got up and grinned down at Frankie. 'Better go and show
everyone how brilliant we are at cricket,' he said. 'Come on!'

He strolled towards the knot of people on the beach and
Frankie sighed as she put the Thermos flask and mugs back
in the basket. Had Jack been trying to tell her that no one could
replace Sue in his or his daughter's life? She shrugged.
Perhaps she was reading too much into his remarks after all.
She started to follow Jack across the sand and Abby ran up to
her and grabbed her hand.

'Hurry up, Frankie,' she urged. 'I've been waiting for you
to come and play.'

'I'm not very good.' Frankie laughed. 'Do you still want me?'

Abby looked up at her in surprise. ''Course I want you,' she
said earnestly. 'I want you to play with us all the afternoon!'

A little glimmer of light seemed to dance in Frankie's mind as she stood as an outfielder. It seemed that Abby was perfectly happy to accept her—now all she had to do was convince the little girl's father that he needed her, too!

The cricket was in full swing when Frankie joined the group. Jack had been asked to bowl to a young boy who played with great concentration. Jack looked very impressive as he made his run-up, his loose T-shirt billowing around him and his battered safari shorts showing off strong, tanned legs. Everyone scattered when the young boy dealt with the first ball in a peremptory fashion, hitting it hard towards the sea near Frankie. She picked it up and hurled it as hard as she could to Jack while the young boy and his playing partner scampered up and down between the wickets. They were so busy looking at where the ball was that they collided as they were running, causing everyone involved to burst into laughter. There was so much noise, in fact, that no one heard the sand yacht come racing towards them.

At the last moment Frankie noticed the red and blue sail come across her line of vision, and then with horror saw that it was completely out of control and heading like a bullet towards Abby. It was too late to shout even if Abby could have heard her above the waves and the general noise of people enjoying themselves. There was a sickening thud and a scream, and as if in slow motion Frankie saw the yacht tip over and scrape along on its side, the occupant being flung out. Abby's little figure was knocked flying in the air like a rag doll, landing a few feet away from the yacht and lying deathly still on the sand.

CHAPTER EIGHT

THE SILENCE FROM the onlookers seemed to go on for ever, although it could only have been a few seconds, Frankie aware only of the swish of the surf on the sand, the mewing of a seagull overhead. Then some of the horrified onlookers started screaming and Frankie found herself running towards the broken little body as fast as she could, her heart almost bursting with the effort.

'Let her be alive, oh, God, let her be alive,' she whispered to herself as she dropped down beside the child and felt for the carotid artery in Abby's neck. There was still a pulse but the little girl looked deathly pale, and from her leg a jet of blood pumped out, staining the sand around a deep red.

'Is she…?' Jack knelt beside Frankie, and looked down at his daughter, his face a terrible grey colour, his voice a barely audible croak. 'I…I can hardly bear to look…'

'She's still with us, Jack,' said Frankie, forcing her voice to sound calm, willing her hands not to tremble as she pulled a handkerchief from her jeans pocket and bound it tightly around the injured leg. 'Hold that leg for me in an elevated position,' she added tersely. She was back in A and E mode, brusque, almost snappy, forcing Jack to react, although he was in shock, and hardly hearing what she said. 'Have you got your mobile on you? Give it to me, please.'

Automatically he reached into his shorts pocket and handed her the phone.

'Tell them it's urgent,' he whispered, tenderly holding his little girl's leg upwards so that the pressure of the blood in the artery was lessened.

Frankie stabbed out the numbers and spoke into the phone, her voice clear and concise. 'We need two blue light ambulances to the Silver Sands Beach. A child of four has been knocked down by a sand yacht and needs urgent attention—possible skull fracture and an arterial bleed in the leg. Medical attention also needed for the driver of the yacht. I'm Dr Lovatt from Denniston Vale A and E Department. Would you inform A and E to have a paediatric neurologist on standby?'

Frankie turned to the crowd that had gathered in horrified silence round them. 'Perhaps you could all give Abby and her father some space?' she asked kindly but firmly.

'Shouldn't we start mouth-to-mouth resuscitation?' asked someone. 'Perhaps give the little girl a drink of water?'

'Yes, she should be moved to somewhere more comfortable,' chimed in another man.

Frankie stood up. 'Jack and I both happen to be doctors,' she explained, her voice authoritative and brisk. 'Abby's breathing by herself, so although she's obviously injured, she is coping at the moment. We don't know the extent of her injuries, so we shouldn't move her in case we exacerbate them.'

'I've had some Red Cross training,' said one woman rather shyly. 'If I can do anything…'

'You can apply some pressure to Abby's leg injury—that would help in slowing the bleed. And I wonder if someone could get me a rug to put over her?' She glanced across to where the yacht lay and by the side of it a youth stood staring at them all. 'I'll go and have a look at the young man by the yacht in a minute.'

Some of the spectators hurried to do as she'd suggested and the others moved respectfully to a distance. Frankie turned her attention back to Abby. She bent low over her and said clearly, 'Abby! Abby! Daddy's here. Where does it hurt, darling?'

Abby's eyelids fluttered for a second and Frankie and Jack's eyes met, a desperate hope flickering in both of them.

'She can hear me, at any rate,' murmured Frankie. She put a comforting hand on Jack's arm. 'Maybe she's OK…'

Jack shook his head, his eyes anguished. 'How can she be? After something like that hitting her, she could have fractured her skull…and I don't want to think of anything else that could be injured.'

Frankie looked closely at the child's nose and ears. 'At the moment there's no sign of a leakage of cerebrospinal fluid,' she said. 'But you know we can't tell anything for certain yet. At least I've seen her move her legs.'

Frankie covered the little girl with a rug someone brought, and Jack stroked Abby's hair gently while still propping up her leg at an angle. 'I'm here, darling,' he whispered. 'I won't leave you…'

The girl helping with Abby's leg seemed to be very competent so Frankie decided to have a quick look at the youth who'd been in the sand yacht.

'I won't be a minute,' she said to Jack. She turned round

and ran quickly towards where the young man was standing. He was deathly pale and shaking. 'How is the little girl?' he whispered. 'I didn't mean for this to happen, I swear. It was a sudden gust of wind sent the thing careering off course.' He put his head in his hands and began to sob brokenly. 'I'm sorry…so sorry…'

Frankie glanced across at Jack, still gazing fixedly at his daughter, then drew the young man further away from Abby and her father. She didn't think that now was the time the two should be introduced. She patted the boy's shoulder comfortingly.

'Sit over here,' she said gently. 'You've had a terrible shock, I know.' She looked at the boy carefully, noting the pallor of his skin, the trembling of his hands and mouth. 'Did you hurt yourself when you fell out of the yacht?' she asked.

'I…don't know,' he muttered. 'I don't know what happened. I think I hurt my back—it's numb.'

'Let me see.' Frankie pulled up the boy's T-shirt and drew in her breath. The skin on his back had been torn back like a wrinkled glove and embedded in it were millions of particles of sand.

'What's your name?' she asked gently.

'Dan…Dan Whiting,' he said wretchedly.

'Well, Dan, you'll need to go to hospital, too,' she said. 'Your back needs cleaning and dressing—and you need to be treated for shock. Sit down beside me until the paramedics get here.'

In the distance they could hear the whine of the ambulance sirens as the vehicles tore along the shore road and in another minute several paramedics in their fluorescent green jackets were running across the sand to where Abby lay. Frankie closed her eyes for a moment in relief—every minute counted when a child had a head injury.

The paramedics were calm and efficient, listening to Frankie's description of the accident and her assessment of Abby's injuries, as far as she was able to give it. Then they took over the situation in a brisk but unflappable manner that gave Jack a few minutes to get his emotions under control, so that by the time they had put a neck collar on the little girl and strapped her to a stiff stretcher, he was able to smile at his daughter and even joke with her a little about Brindle.

'Brindle's been sitting next to you all the time,' he told Abby. 'He's been telling the ambulance men what happened.'

Abby's eyes flickered open. 'Good old Brindle,' she whispered.

The medics began to carry the little figure back across the sands to the ambulances waiting on the road, and the crew from the second ambulance were dealing with Dan Whiting.

'I'll bring your car to the hospital,' said Frankie to Jack. 'Do you want me to tell your mother? I can go over to her ward and explain what's happened.'

Jack gave a twisted smile. 'At least she's in the same place as Abby and not in some hospital thirty miles away.' He looked bleakly at Frankie. 'And, yes, I'd be grateful if you'd drive the car and I'll go with Abby.'

He looked so grim, so alone. Frankie could almost hear him thinking that Sue should be with him to share in the worry and agony of their child's accident. Impetuously she put her arms round his bowed shoulders and hugged him. She didn't say anything because any words she chose would be useless—they had no idea how much Abby was hurt and what damage had been done. All she could offer Jack was the physical comfort of knowing that she was there if he needed her.

'I'll see you in the hospital,' she promised. She nearly said, 'Try not to worry.' But that was the kind of banal phrase one said to patients to calm and reassure them—it would mean nothing to Jack who knew the consequences of such an accident only too well.

He gripped her arm for a moment. 'Thanks…yes, I'd like you to be with me.'

And then he was gone, striding over the beach behind the little party of medics taking his daughter to A and E.

It was a long night. A hospital at night-time is rather a spooky place with a different atmosphere to that during the day, reflected Frankie as she made her way to the children's ward where Abby had been taken. The corridors were quiet, harshly lit with neon lights, the wards dark, sometimes a pool of light above a bed as a nurse attended to a very sick patient. Abby was lying in her own little bay, hooked up to various instruments monitoring her blood pressure, her heart rate and giving her liquids to combat the loss of fluid she'd sustained from the trauma of the accident. By her bed sat Jack, his head bowed, looking very weary. He looked up when Frankie appeared and smiled.

'Thanks for coming, Frankie. The good news is that the scan didn't show any bleeds or, thank God, a skull fracture. They think it was probably a glancing blow that hit her side.'

'What a relief,' breathed Frankie, sitting on the other side of the bed and stroking the little hand that lay on the sheet. 'What's the bad news, then?'

'She didn't lose too much blood from that gash, thanks to you, and she's got a simple fracture of the tibia. She's going to be in a cast for a few weeks—but if that's all that she's done, she's got off very lightly.' He passed a weary hand over his face. 'I don't mind telling you I've been imagining all kinds of things…'

His voice trailed off and Frankie looked at him sympathetically. 'Of course you have—and so have I. What you need is a very strong cup of tea or coffee—and I'm going to get you one now.'

She marched away to the A and E department, where the first person she saw was Sister Kenney.

'I've come to steal some of that freshly ground coffee you keep in the staff cupboard for Jack,' she said. 'I think he needs more than the machine-made sludge at the moment!'

'How's Jack's little girl?' Sister Kenney asked as they walked to the staffroom. 'Poor child—any test results yet? We couldn't believe it was his daughter that was brought in.'

'No intracranial bleeding shown up,' said Frankie. 'That's such a relief. Her leg's broken, but hopefully that's the worst injury.'

Sister Kenney went to a filing cabinet and pulled out a small bottle. 'Put a slug of this in it.' Her normally stern face relaxed into a conspiratorial grin. 'I keep a little brandy here just in case—purely medicinal, you understand. As long as Jack's not driving, it might help to steady his nerves!'

Frankie went back to Jack and thrust the fortified coffee into his hand. 'This is with love from Sister Kenney—she assures me it'll do you a power of good!'

Jack took a swallow of the coffee and for the first time for a few hours a grin spread over his face. 'Just what the doctor ordered. Now, sit down with me for a while. I want to know what happened to the young man in the sand yacht.'

'They're keeping him in—he may need a skin graft on his back. He's very shocked and devastated by what happened. Of course, the police are going to interview him.'

'What a difference a few minutes make,' said Jack grimly. 'One minute everyone was enjoying a lovely afternoon, the next the whole day had changed.'

'It could have been worse,' said Frankie softly.

Jack leaned forward towards her and took her hands. 'You were wonderful, Frankie. If it hadn't been for you getting to Abby so quickly and stopping that bleed in her leg, it could have been a very different story. I shall never forget it...'

The staff nurse came up to the bay. 'I wish I could persuade you to go and have a sleep,' she said to Jack. 'Abby's sedated anyway and it would do you a lot of good.'

'I'm not leaving this hospital,' said Jack grimly. 'I wouldn't be able to sleep in case she needed me.'

'There's a spare room just at the end of the corridor that the junior doctors use when they're on call,' suggested the nurse. 'Why don't you take that? We can come and wake you as soon as Abby comes round and needs you.'

'A brilliant idea,' said Frankie. 'You've been on the go since you brought your mother in last night and you need the rest.'

Jack stood up reluctantly and stretched. 'OK, but you promise you'll let me know immediately—'

'Promise.' The nurse smiled.

'I'll go home now,' Frankie said. She yawned and flicked

a look at her watch. 'I'm due back in a few hours so I need to get to bed.'

She and Jack walked down the corridor together, and stopped at the door of the on-call room.

'I'm tired,' he said. 'But I don't think I'll get a wink of sleep.' He paused and took her hand, drawing her closer to him. 'You were a star,' he whispered. 'Thank you, Frankie.'

The area was only dimly lit, and in the half-light his eyes were dark, the outline of his profile showing his straight nose and strong jawline. With his other hand he took off his glasses and she saw the gleam of his teeth as he smiled.

'These are a damn nuisance when you're around,' he murmured, then he pulled her against him and kissed her full on her lips. 'Perhaps I shouldn't do this when we said we wouldn't get too…intimate, but, hell, Frankie, if you hadn't been there for me today I would have found it very very difficult. It's made me realise just how much I need you…want you…'

Those words were nice to hear, Frankie thought, but that's not quite the same as love…they'd both needed each other at difficult times, but she'd been the one to fall like a ton of bricks for him.

'I'll do anything I can to help,' she murmured. 'You know how fond I am of Abby.'

'You can help me tonight,' he said huskily. 'I know what we agreed…' his hands tightened round her '…but, please, stay with me for a while—it's the only way I'll calm down and get some sleep.'

He opened the door, still holding onto Frankie's hand, and pulled her into the room with him.

'Lie down beside me, Frankie...' His arms were still around her and there was an urgent pleading in his voice.

Was it madness to give in to him? Her heart pounded in anticipation at what they were about to do. But Jack had been through a lot today—why shouldn't she comfort him? And if it was only the comfort of sex he wanted then she was going to ignore all the warnings good sense told her to heed. He really wanted Sue, she thought sadly, but Sue wasn't around and she was, and she could at least pretend that he loved her, couldn't she?

'If anyone comes in, they'll get a surprise,' she whispered.

'I've locked the door,' he murmured, and in the dark she heard him chuckle—at least he'd cheered up a little since the events of the afternoon.

With a sigh she turned towards him and gently he started to undo the buttons on the shirt she'd still got on from the after-noon at the beach. Then he slipped his hands round her back and unhooked her bra, and in the half-light of the room her breasts spilled out, the soft creamy skin showing white in the muted light. He put his lips down to their soft curves and kissed them with gentle butterfly kisses, then with an exclamation of impatience tore off his T-shirt and pressed his hard body to hers.

'God, you feel beautiful, Frankie. Your skin's so soft, like a peach,' he said huskily. His hands slid down to her jeans, unzipping them, and she wriggled out of them, kicking them off, so that those hands could explore the most intimate part of her body, rousing her to fever pitch, his lips fluttering over the hollow in her neck. And in return she kissed his chest, his neck and his face. They tumbled onto the bed and he looked for a long minute at her naked body, the shadows from the windows flickering over it. Then he lay on top of her, his smooth skin against hers, and she answered his demanding body, feeling a sense of happiness for him when he sank upon her at last, murmuring incoherent thanks.

In another second he was asleep, his body curled around hers and totally relaxed.

Frankie looked up at the ceiling and sighed. It had been wonderful—passionate, thrilling—but almost silent love-making. She twisted round to look at his peaceful face, listened to his gentle breathing and felt a sense of compassion as well as love for this man who had experienced so much sadness in his life. Today, when he'd thought he might lose his child as well as his wife, must have been too terrible to contemplate.

Carefully she eased herself away from his muscular body and started to get dressed. Perhaps one day he would come to love her, but for the time being she would have to be content with the fact that he'd said he needed her.

The week wore on and as usual Casualty was very busy—although there were times when there was a lull in the day or the evening and Frankie would find herself longing for Jack to come over and talk to her. After their tumultuous evening together in the hospital after Abby's accident, Frankie could not stop thinking about Jack, rerunning the scene over and over in her mind, hoping to see him, hoping that he'd ask her out. The truth was, she didn't know where she stood with him. He'd said he needed her, but if that was so, why no phone call or contact of any kind? Of course he was worried about his mother and Abby, but from her own enquiries and visits she knew that both of them were improving rapidly. Abby was being kept in to monitor her head wound but, apart from the cast on her leg, looked much better.

Damn the man! thought Frankie bitterly as she pushed some papers savagely into a file. I'm not going to let him drift away from me—just use me when he feels the need. He may still hanker after Sue, but I'm ready to move on now and forget the past. Why can't he?

Bob Richards, one of the staff nurses, tapped her on the shoulder. 'Frankie, you're wanted in cubicle five. A female aged twenty-four with a most peculiar thing on her jaw— looks like a sort of boil with a hard centre.'

'Sounds nasty. What's her name?'

'Angela Cummings—and I've got to say she's a cracker.'

Frankie wagged an admonitory finger at him. 'Now, now Bob, less of that.'

Bob was right—the girl was extremely beautiful, her hair long and glossy like a blonde sheet of silk, a figure to die for and large brown eyes like a fawn's, with long eyelashes. She clutched a handbag, fiddling nervously with the strap as she waited for Frankie to take her history.

'I don't like to bother you and it's probably nothing serious.' She spoke rapidly betraying how worried she really was.

'Do you remember injuring your face?' asked Frankie as she looked closely at the lesion on the girl's cheek.

'No—I'd have remembered if I had done. It…it started a few weeks ago,' the girl said in a breathy voice. 'I thought it was a spot—it was red, and then it changed. Sort of turned in on itself and developed a hard piece in the middle—it looks weird. And now I can't disguise it with make-up…'

Her voice trailed off and she bit her lip to stop it trembling.

Frankie used a penlight to peer at the girl's cheek between her ear and mouth. The lesion resembled a ruptured boil with a hard grey centre and an inflamed border.

'Is it painful?' she asked.

'It has been—it doesn't hurt so much now. But the thing is, I'm a photographic model—it's really important that my face looks OK. I know they can airbrush blemishes, but this looks awful, very difficult to disguise…' The girl's voice faltered. 'I know it's silly, but I'm frightened it could be, you know, a sort of…tumour.'

She brought the last word out in a rush, as if the very saying of it was dangerous.

'You're not being silly at all,' Frankie assured her. 'I'll be honest, I've never seen anything quite like it. It looks like a sort of boil, but I don't think it is. I'd like to get a colleague in to look at it.'

She went out of the cubicle and towards the central desk where Jack and Tim were deep in discussion.

'You've got to help me out with this one,' Tim was saying, looking mournfully at Jack. 'I've got to find one more player. You're my only hope…'

'When is the match?' asked Jack warily.

'This Saturday—we've got to beat St Mary's this time. We can't do that with just ten men.'

'OK, but I'm no premiership footballer.'

'Don't worry—I'll put you in goal,' declared Tim. He swung off down the corridor, humming happily to himself.

'I don't know what I've let myself in for,' said Jack to Frankie. 'It's years since I played football, and I don't like the sound of being a goalie much!'

His eyes flickered over her and he made as if to say something and then shook his head slightly, before saying briskly. 'Can I help?'

'I've got a photographic model in cubicle three,' Frankie said.

'Sounds good so far.' He grinned.

She wrinkled her nose at him. 'She's a very worried photographic model,' she added. 'And I must say I don't blame her—I don't know what to make of it myself. She's got the most peculiar boil on her face. It's wrinkled around the edges and indurated, and has something like a stone in the centre.'

'A stone?' repeated Jack. 'Perhaps it's a large diamond—people put them in their navels, don't they? Or perhaps it's a blackhead she's been trying to squeeze. I bet she's got herself into a state because of a small blemish.'

'You come and look at it—see what you think. It looks more than a blemish to me.'

In the cubicle Angela was sitting nervously bolt upright and touching her cheek. 'I think the hard bit's got bigger,' she said quaveringly. 'I know it's a kind of growth, and I'll lose my job. I know it sounds awful, but my face is my fortune…'

Jack looked at her perceptively. It wasn't hard to tell that the young woman was terrified. He smiled kindly at her and said in his calm way, 'Don't let's jump to conclusions—let's not worry before we have to, eh?'

Frankie watched the girl relax. How often she had seen the effect he had on frightened patients—that combination of authority and kindness that soothed and comforted them. He bent forward and swung the anglepoise lamp on the wall so that the full light played on the lesion. Then he gave a little grunt of surprise.

'You know what? I saw this kind of thing not two months ago…' He picked up a steel probe from the instrument tray. 'Don't worry—this won't hurt,' he assured Angela.

She held her breath and closed her eyes as he tapped the stone-like middle of the lesion. It felt as hard as cement.

'Did you feel that?' he asked the girl.

'No—it's sort of numb.' She looked at him tensely. 'You've found something horrible haven't you?'

Big brown eyes brimmed with tears as she looked up at him, and Jack smiled and folded his arms. 'You can stop worrying. I know it looks very ominous, but I have to tell you there's nothing sinister about it at all…'

Frankie looked enquiringly at him. 'You've got an idea what it is?'

'Not just an idea—I know what it is.' He grinned. 'What she's been worrying about is a stray wisdom tooth that's quietly been growing through her jaw and has just erupted in the last few days!'

Both Frankie and Angela looked at him in amazement. 'A wisdom tooth? Is that really it?' Angela said haltingly. 'No cancer?'

'No cancer—it just needs to be removed. What you can see is the crown beginning to appear.'

'Of course!' said Frankie. 'Now I look at it again, I can see what you mean. That's pretty amazing, for the tooth to be working its way to the surface all that time and you didn't know it!'

Angela's face went through several emotions at once as she laughed and wiped her eyes at the same time. 'I feel so relieved,' she hiccuped.

'The tooth fairy works in mysterious ways,' said Jack with a grin. He scribbled something on a piece of paper and handed it to Angela. 'Take this to Reception and they'll give you an appointment at the dental clinic for them to remove it. Worries over!'

'I'm so grateful. Thank you both so much. I really thought. Oh, well, my days of photographic modelling aren't over, then!'

Angela went out of the room, clutching the piece of paper to her like a talisman, looking as if she'd won the lottery.

'Wow! Who'd have thought that a tooth would come through like that?' said Frankie. 'I'd almost convinced myself it was malignant.'

They walked back towards the desk together. Frankie flicked a glance towards Jack. Had he been thinking of her at all? Did their passionate night ever cross his mind? She cleared her throat, damned if she was going to let things slide.

'I'm glad Abby's so much better—I went to see her at lunchtime and she was tucking into her food.'

If it was a hint, he didn't rise to the bait, merely remarking, 'Thank God, yes. And my mother was discharged today, so hopefully when Abby is allowed home she can go back to the farm until she's allowed back to school.'

And that was all. No mention of how much he'd needed her that night after the accident, or the sweet comfort he'd said she'd given him. Frankie swallowed and walked more quickly, determined that she wasn't going to allow another man to rock her life like Damian had. Yes, she was the one who'd told Jack to keep things cool between them, but surely after that last passionate episode he might just mention it!

There was no one at the desk and Frankie sat down with

angry tears stinging her eyes. It did nothing for her temper to realise that she'd allowed herself to be used again—had fallen for someone who'd sweet-talked her into bed with him. The first time they'd made love there had been exceptional circumstances—now she seemed to be making a habit of it. More fool her, she thought bitterly.

She leant back in the chair for a moment, her eyes closed and the scene from their night together flashed into her mind with vivid reality. She could almost feel his hard body driving against hers, his demanding lips and hands fluttering over her until she was driven wild. Whenever she thought of him she came alive, her heartbeat quickened and every nerve end felt as if a small electric charge had gone through it. But, of course, it had only been a comfort thing hadn't it? Something, she thought painfully and with a little quirk of her lips, to help him sleep.

'If he hasn't even got the decency to refer to the evening, if it meant completely nothing to him, I'll have to be less free and easy with my favours,' she muttered to herself as she started trying to sort out the blood-test results that had arrived back in the department for the relevant patients. No way was she going to allow herself to be humiliated again just because she'd fallen for the most gorgeous man in the hospital. He was going to have to work pretty hard if he wanted her to go with him again, she thought grimly. Then perhaps if she played hard to get he'd start thinking of her as more than a comfort blanket.

'You've not forgotten the conference tomorrow, have you?' Sister Kenney's voice cut though her thoughts. 'Apparently they're still trying to find cover for you and Jack Herrick. I guess,' she added gloomily, 'it will be chaos here without you.'

She stumped off crossly and Frankie reflected that it would

be difficult for her, too, spending the day with a man who treated her as if she'd been a shot of barbiturate or a hot-water bottle.

She gave a little gasp of surprise as a hand cupped her chin and tipped her face upwards. She found herself looking into Jack's eyes.

'Sorry to disturb you, Doctor, but I must speak to you rather urgently.'

Frankie scowled at him, disguising her shock that the very man she had been daydreaming about was only five inches away from her. Whatever he wanted, she wasn't going to be won over by gorgeous blue eyes.

'If it's about a locum registrar for tomorrow when we're at that day conference, I've been told they haven't been able to get anyone yet.'

He smiled. 'Oh, that's been sorted now. It's something even more urgent. You must wonder why I haven't been in touch.'

She almost tossed her head disdainfully, but kept her eyes averted from his. 'Not at all, Jack. I've been much too busy to think about things like that.'

He raised an eyebrow. 'Really? You haven't thought about the other night together at all?'

His look was penetrating, disbelieving, and a tell-tale blush spread over Frankie's cheeks.

'Well…I know you've been busy,' she said rather feebly.

He leaned forward, his hands on the desk, his stethoscope swinging an inch from her nose. 'Not too busy to obliterate what happened that night, sweetheart.' he said huskily. 'I just haven't been able to see you alone. And that's what I want to do. Tomorrow there'll be an opportunity to be by ourselves.

Let me give you a lift tomorrow to the conference, then we can grab a bite to eat together on the way back…please.'

Play hard to get? Cool it? Frankie felt her virtuous intentions vaporise and a rush of happiness made her stomach flutter with excitement.

'I'd love to,' she said.

CHAPTER NINE

'I DON'T USUALLY look forward to these conferences,' remarked Jack as they set off on the main road out of Denniston Vale. 'But this time I can't wait.'

Frankie looked across at him impishly. 'Of course you're looking forward to it—eradication of hospital-borne infections is very important.'

He grinned. 'I'm not denying I want to know more about it…'

'I'm sure you'll find it extremely interesting.'

He grimaced. 'Dammit, you know that's not what I mean. If you want me to spell it out, it's because I can spend some time with you alone.'

His glance flicked across to her and their eyes met in an electrical charge of attraction that sent a shiver of anticipation through Frankie's body. She bit her lip. This time, however much she wanted it, there was to be no leaping into bed together. It seemed that each time they'd made love, it had been she who'd fallen deeper and deeper for Jack, while he had treated it as something therapeutic rather than romantic.

'We may find every minute's taken up,' she said.

'Well, we're not having dinner with everyone else,' he

growled. 'As I said yesterday, we'll go out for a bite to eat by ourselves. I'll have given enough of my time to medical matters by the end of the day.'

The conference was being held at a large country house hotel about half an hour's drive from Denniston Vale. It was set in the grounds of beautiful parkland, with magnificent beech trees forming an arch over a long drive to the stately home it once had been. In front of the hotel a large lake glittered in the sun and a pair of swans glided across the surface.

'This looks pretty classy,' Jack remarked as he got out of the car and handed Frankie her briefcase. 'Let's hope the lectures aren't too long and we can go for a walk in the grounds.'

'I wouldn't bank on it,' said Frankie as they walked into the hotel.

As it happened, the audience were informed that the afternoon speaker had been held up at an airport and his lecture was cancelled—they had the rest of the afternoon to themselves.

'Hallelujah! What a result!' exulted Jack. 'Let's take the opportunity to stretch our legs. I don't seem to have been out of the hospital for days. Now my mother and Abby are so much better, I feel as if I've been let out of school!'

Frankie was silent. It sounded just what she wanted, wasn't it? A bracing walk with a man she loved. But, then, he didn't love her, and he was unaware that she had fallen for him. She'd given him the impression on the day she'd found out about Damian that she didn't want any ties, and Jack was probably very happy with that arrangement. She had no doubt that if there were just two of them alone on this walk, they would kiss each other—and probably more. She shivered with anticipation. She would have to use every ounce of will power to keep him at arm's length.

Jack was looking at her quizzically. 'A penny for them? You look a bit doubtful.'

They were standing in the great hall of the hotel with people bustling around them, all talking, laughing, speaking on mobiles.

'I'm frightened to come with you, Jack,' Frankie whispered.

'You're what?' he asked, putting his head down to hear her better.

She took a deep breath and said in a louder voice, 'I'm frightened we're getting into a dangerous habit for two people who don't want to have ties or get involved...'

There was a lull in the noise of the hall and her voice seemed to her to echo loudly and embarrassingly from wall to wall. Several people stared at her as they walked past.

Jack took her arm. 'I think we ought to talk about this on our walk,' he said gravely, piloting her out of the door.

They started walking along the path around the lake, which led into a wood some way away from the hotel. They were very close to each other but not touching, for Jack had dropped his hand from her arm, and yet the atmosphere between them crackled like a newly lit fire. One touch was all it would take, thought Frankie, looking straight ahead. One touch for her to do anything Jack wanted her to do. How wonderful it would be to lie on the ground here, with the sun filtering through the trees and dappling the ground with shafts of light streaming through the branches... Frankie took a deep breath and inhaled the earthy smell of leaves and damp earth.

'Mmm…lovely,' she sighed. 'I'd forgotten how sweet every-thing smells in the country.' She looked across at him and suddenly decided she didn't want to talk about their relation-ship now. She just wanted a country walk with no complications.

'It was a good talk this morning on MRSA, wasn't it?' she said brightly.

Jack didn't reply directly, but kept striding on purposefully as if thinking, then he stopped in his tracks and said suddenly, 'What did you mean, Frankie, about being frightened of getting into dangerous habits?'

Frankie swallowed. She was caught between the devil and the deep blue sea, she thought wryly.

'For goodness' sake, Jack, let's enjoy the walk. I don't know what I meant really…'

He gripped her arm and swung her round to face him. 'Of course you know. For heaven's sake, are we never to have an adult conversation?'

He wasn't going to let it pass. Frankie sighed. 'I suppose I meant that…'

'Yes?' he prompted, looking at her intently, his gaze sweeping over her heart-shaped face and her wide, troubled eyes. 'Let me guess—you don't want us to make love again, is that it?'

Frankie almost laughed. Not want to make love to Jack? Her knees were weak with a longing for him to crush her in his arms, for their bodies to meld together once more in glorious passion. She looked down at the ground for a second, a rosy blush creeping over her cheeks. Then she threw back her head and looked at him with challenging eyes, her hands on her hips as if she'd made a big decision.

Taking a deep breath, she said in a rush, 'OK. I do want to make love—but not at the expense of my heart, Jack. You see, you're beginning to mean more to me than I realised—in fact, I think I might be a little in love with you. I can't do passion and keep a light-hearted friendship.'

Jack blinked as if he couldn't believe what he'd heard, and Frankie flashed a look of embarrassed impatience at him. 'Oh, for God's sake, surely you understand? I've been dumped by one man I adored—I don't want to end up adoring someone else. It…it makes you too vulnerable.'

He gave a twisted little smile. 'I'm not a complete idiot—of course I understand. You told me you wanted to be a free spirit with no commitments. And you were right to want that, Frankie. After loving Damian for so long, I think you need space to get over him—not to rebound into another relationship.'

'But I don't love Damian now…'

'It must have left a scar—you were engaged for a long time.'

'I know that,' she said angrily. 'But that was in the past. I'm ready to move on.'

He sighed heavily. 'I wish I could see the future more clearly.' He put his hands on her shoulders and looked down at her with compassion. 'You see I come with a lot of baggage, a little girl who's lost a beloved mother… It wouldn't be fair to lumber you with that.'

And there was a wife who could never be replaced, thought Frankie sadly. She looked away from him, feeling humiliated and foolish. Now she'd told him she loved him but he'd kept his own feelings for her under wraps—a casual affair was obviously all he wanted.

It was as if he was reading her mind. His arms moved from

her shoulders to her waist and he pulled her towards him, lowering his face to hers. 'Francesca, sweetheart, I told you once that I think of you as my best friend—you're more than that now. When we make love together it's the most glorious thing in the world—but I don't want to hurt you. If you want to put things on a platonic basis then I'll do that.' His eyes twinkled into hers. 'But it'll be damn difficult…'

What should she say? Finish everything and treat Jack as she would any other colleague? Impossible to contemplate, because Jack was too close to her. They had become too intimate to go back now and she knew it. She drew his head down to hers and he took her lips with his in a gentle, lingering kiss.

'That was the answer I hoped you'd give,' he whispered, and he smiled down at her. 'I don't want you to think that every time we've made love it's because I've needed sex as some sort of therapy…'

Frankie felt the colour rise in her cheeks—that was just what she had thought sometimes. 'We…we've both been under strain, emotionally hurt and vulnerable. It seemed the natural thing to fall into each other's arms,' she offered cautiously.

He turned her head up to his and looked at her with those deep azure eyes. 'I wasn't doing it solely because of that, sweetheart,' he said huskily. 'I was making love to you because I feel so much for you—and I have done for a very long time.'

She stared at him in confusion. 'You love me?' she said stupidly.

'Of course I do,' he said softly.

The little flutter of happiness that Frankie's heart gave

gradually became a thudding drum roll of ecstasy. He'd said he loved her—actually admitted it! She felt dizzy with joy. It bubbled up in a rush of laughter and she wound her arms around his neck and pressed her body close to his.

'Tell me again,' she whispered in his ear.

He smiled and held her away from him for a moment. 'I love you, Francesca, I want to be with you—and I want to make love to you whenever I am with you.'

The world spun round Frankie in a crescendo of happiness. The birds seemed to be singing more joyfully, even the rustle of the leaves in the trees were like chuckles of laughter. She laughed up at him, any questions she'd had about his feelings for her fading away. There were questions she still needed to have answers to, but now she was too overcome, too entranced to ask them.

Her eyes laughed up at him. 'You say you want to make love to me whenever you're with me? Well, you're with me now, Jack Herrick,' she said boldly, 'and we're all alone.'

'So we are…'

They stared at each other for a second, as if suddenly realising that they'd crossed a momentous Rubicon, then his fingers started to undo the buttons of her shirt impatiently and he pulled the shirt from her, bending his head to kiss the soft flesh of her curving breasts spilling out of the constraints of her bra.

'My God,' he breathed. 'How I've longed to do this all day…'

He pulled her down onto the dry leaves under the tall beech trees and unhooked her skirt, pulling it away so that she lay before him in just her bra and pants. And then in a blur of impatience she pulled them off to help him and started to undo the button of his trouser waistband. They both laughed as he kicked his trousers off and then he was lying on top of her, his warm flesh covering hers, his hands stroking first her breasts and then slipping down between her legs, driving her to fever pitch with the insistent exploration of her body with delicate fingers. She murmured in ecstasy, longing for him to enter her, and rays from the sun shining through the branches above them dappled Jack's strong face as he looked down at her with a most tender expression.

'You are so beautiful, my darling. You smell so sweet— your hair, your skin. I could eat you up!'

His mouth teased her lips open then started to kiss her breasts and stomach with butterfly lightness, so that she wriggled beneath him with the sheer joy of making love with someone who loved her. When he became more demanding, his need overcoming his gentleness, she echoed his passion and they rode the storm of rapture together until, both satiated, they fell back on the leaves beside each other.

They were both silent for a while, then they turned to look at each other, a curving smile on each of their faces. Jack levered himself up on one arm and stroked her hair.

'That wasn't bad, was it?' he said. 'I think with a lot of practice we'll do it perfectly!'

Frankie giggled and sat up. 'I've got leaves in the most extraordinary places…'

He pulled her down against him. 'We'll attend to that later. As I said, let's get in some more practice while we can!'

She looked at him with wide eyes. 'Now?'

'No time like the present, my love…'

'Oh, all right, then,' she murmured, moving her body sensually against his. 'Show me what you mean…'

Corey was sitting in the staffroom with her legs over the arm of a chair, grabbing the opportunity to put her feet up. She bit into a large cream bun and swept her gaze over Frankie, pouring coffee by the sink.

'This bun's delicious. How many calories would you say it has in it?'

'About three thousand,' said Frankie, putting a cup of coffee by Corey's chair. 'I thought you were on a diet?'

Corey made a face. 'It's only the one bun. Anyway, no matter how I try, I'll never be as slender as you. By the way, how was the conference yesterday?'

'Quite good,' said Frankie casually, but her heart raced as she thought of the afternoon she'd spent with Jack. 'I brought back a load of literature and we're having a hospital meeting about it all next week.'

A mischievous smile lit Corey's face. 'I thought you might find it a bit of a bore—but, then, you did have the gorgeous Dr Herrick with you, so I expect that made up for things…'

'I don't know what you mean by that,' said Frankie primly, keeping her face turned away from the observant Corey. 'He gave me a lift and that was all really…'

Frankie felt a zing of happiness flooding through her as it had at intervals all day. She loved and was loved—and by the most wonderful man. It seemed extraordinary that they had worked together for so long without any hint of attraction— but, of course, she'd thought she'd been in love with Damian then. Now there was something like gratitude in her attitude to Damian—if he hadn't broken off their engagement, she might never have fallen for Jack. Now her thoughts were a jumbled mixture of happiness and excitement for the future.

The sudden insistent clamour of the general alert bell made both women jump—indeed, most of the staff who were making the most of a lull in admissions were startled. Tim dropped a stack of chairs he was carrying with a crash, and Jack hit his head on an open cupboard door as he straightened up from examining a patient. Frankie and Corey made their way to the office immediately—the alert bell was a warning to all Casualty personnel to gather before an emergency alert.

They all crowded into the office, Jack rubbing his forehead ruefully. His glance flicked across to Frankie and he gave her a conspiratorial little smile. She grinned back at him.

'What's up?' he asked Sister Kenney.

'There's been a house fire on the outskirts of Denniston, probably caused by a gas explosion,' she informed them briskly. 'There are about six people with serious to minor burns on the way—one of them could be a child. We need to make sure the two theatres are ready and the emergency room's set up. Tim and Nurse Davidson, could you, please, sort out the burns packs, and the rest of the nurses and myself will deal with the theatres. We've got two doctors from Surgical to come in as well.'

Frankie felt her heart sink. Of all the many and varied procedures they had to deal with in Casualty, a burns case was the one she found the most stressful and difficult to deal with. It was an emotional reaction to a horrible and potentially fatal injury that she'd always found difficult to conquer, but she knew she wasn't alone in this. Some people found it hard to cope with other types of injuries and even operations, and only time and experience helped. She took a deep breath to pull herself together, because even now she could hear the whine of the sirens as the ambulances made their way up the drive to the A and E entrance.

In five minutes there was the appearance of chaos as trolleys with recumbent patients on them were trundled quickly to the emergency room for assessment, and staff, already gowned and scrubbed up, circled around them. It was organised chaos, however. Beside each bed in the emergency room were packs of sterile gloves and all the drips and equipment necessary in the treatment of burns cases were set in place.

Frankie swallowed hard as she began on the first of three stages of emergency treatment on a young man with a bad burn to his chest and multiple burns on his arms. If she concentrated on treating the patient and not on the appearance or even the acrid smell of his injury, she could cope. His clothing had been cut away and Frankie first inserted an airway into his throat, flicking a look at the name tag on the bed.

'This is Dermot Lanyon—he's got a respiratory compromise of some kind here,' she said to Jack who was moving between the beds to offer help to any staff who needed it. 'I've managed to draw out some mucus and he is breathing more easily, but we need to keep an eye on him.'

'I'll start off the Ringer's solution,' said Jack, inserting a catheter into the man's shoulder. He turned to Cindy, who was watching the patient's treatment, flicking a glance at her horrified white face. 'This is a wonderful liquid. It replaces vital salts such as sodium, potassium, calcium and chloride, which can be destroyed in a burns accident, as well as replacing lost body fluid.'

His voice was calm and authoritative, bringing the girl back to normality, forcing her to think of how to deal with the present situation by practical means. He knew only too well the effect of seeing a bad burns victim on an inexperienced nurse, and Frankie, drawing off blood for typing and cross-matching, was well aware of what he was doing to alleviate Cindy's distress. Indeed, she could identify with it, although she had learned to control her outward signs of stress. She quickly followed Jack's example.

'We can get a lot of information from the blood I'm taking,' she explained to Cindy. 'Apart from finding out his blood type, we can get a corpuscle count and check his chemical levels. All this will help us when he's being treated. Now, can you ask Nurse Davidson to give him an anti-tetanus injection?'

Cindy whisked out of the room, glad of something to do that would take her away from the terrible sight of the young man's full-depth burn and the brilliant red surface of his chest, patched with strips of slimy detached skin.

'This man needs to go on a ventilator and I'm sending him to ICU pronto when we've put a dressing on his chest and ca-therterised him,' said Frankie, straightening up from taking blood from the patient's arm. 'Tim, give us five minutes and then take Mr Lanyon here to ICU—they've a bed ready.'

Dermot Lanyon had hardly left the room when Sister Kenney came in looking slightly dishevelled, her normally neat hair escaping from its tight knot and her face flushed, be-traying the strain of a sudden emergency on top of the ordinary calls made on the casualty department.

'Can you come and attend to a little girl in the burns room? She's not very badly burned, thank God, but she's very shocked.'

'Better get someone from Paediatrics down,' said Frankie. 'I'd like her wound looked at before we put a dressing on.'

She made her way swiftly to the room specially set aside for burns, although there were too many patients for them all to be treated there at the moment. Dealing with a child who'd been burned was much worse than coping with an adult—she hoped devoutly that Sister Kenney was right and it wasn't a major injury.

The little girl was at the end of the room, her tiny figure dwarfed by the large bed. Incongruously, the child was dressed in a little fairy outfit, complete with wings, and in her hand she still clutched a wand with a star at the end of it. Corey was standing by her, stroking her forehead and talking to her in a low, comforting voice.

'Now, who have we got here?' asked Frankie.

'This is Julie Watts—she's got a poorly leg. But she's being very brave.'

Corey's eyes met Frankie's. They both knew the child was being too good, too quiet. Her whole system was in shock and they would have to try and reverse the process.

Frankie sat down in a chair by Julie and smiled at her. 'You look so beautiful, sweetheart. Are you a fairy?'

Julie nodded, her eyes wide, but her lips trembled. Frankie ran her eyes assessingly over the little patient's arm, which had a long area where the skin was red and blistered. Frankie pulled on some sterile gloves and examined the injury more carefully under the overhead inspection light.

'It's quite a bad partial burn,' she said to Corey. 'Let's get a drip going and I'll take some bloods for an electrolyte count and her blood urea.'

The little girl began to cry softly. 'I want my mummy,' she whispered. 'Where is she?'

'Don't worry, pet, she'll be along soon. We'll go and find her for you when we've looked at your poorly arm.' Frankie looked across at Corey with raised brows and mouthed, 'Do you know where she is?'

Corey shook her head. 'Sister's got a list of the people brought in—that should help us to locate her.' She extracted the wand gently from the child's hand. 'Give me this wand for just a minute, pet, and I'll show you who's going to look after it for you.'

She reached into a cupboard on the wall and took out a large teddy bear, who had done sterling work over the years in reducing young patients' fears, and held the toy up so Julie could see it.

'Look, I'm going to strap the wand to Teddy's paw. He'll be very careful of it, and he'll sit on the cupboard here and be company for you. He's very fond of little boys and girls— he'd like to be your friend.'

All the time Corey was talking and attaching the wand to the bear's paw, Julie watched the toy intently, and when the bear was put inches from her face on the cupboard a little smile lifted the corners of her mouth. She had begun to relax, which was exactly what they had hoped she would do. Corey took the chance to attach a drip to the little girl's other arm.

'There!' she said brightly. 'All done!'

Julie turned and looked at Frankie and Corey. 'I like Teddy,' she whispered.

'Well, then, love,' said Frankie, 'when we've put a dressing on your sore arm and bandaged it up, Teddy can sleep in the bed with you. Would you like that?'

Again the child nodded, but she was more composed now, looking around at the room and the other people in it.

'Soon you'll be going to a room with other children,' explained Frankie. 'It's a lovely room with lots of pictures of animals and fairies on the wall—and Teddy will go with you.'

When Dr Furney, the paediatrician, had inspected Julie's injury, the little girl was taken to the children's ward.

'How did it happen?' he asked Frankie as they went out of the burns room.

'The poor little thing was going to have a birthday party apparently—they were just waiting for the guests and her mother put on the kettle. There's some suggestion that the gas meter was being bypassed in some way and the whole room exploded.'

'Good God,' said Dr. Furney. 'Was she the only child involved?'

'Apparently. If it had happened after the children had all arrived, it doesn't bear thinking about.'

'It's so dangerous to fiddle with gas,' said Dr Furney grimly. 'We've still got a child in the ward who's recovering from a similar incident five weeks ago. Poor little mite.'

'I'd like to know how Julie is, so I'll pop in tomorrow,' said Frankie. 'The trouble with Casualty is that you often don't get to follow up on what happens. Now I'll go and try and find the parents—I presume they were in the building.'

Sister Kenney was nowhere to be seen, so Frankie went up to the whiteboard which listed the admissions and where the patients were located. One of the names was a Tracey Watts, who was being treated in the emergency room. Frankie went in and waited by the woman's bed while her wound was being dressed. Her face had been badly burned but she'd been sedated and was lying quite calmly, allowing the nurses to deal with her.

'I think this is the mother of a young patient I've just been treating,' said Frankie to the doctor looking after Tracey. 'How is Tracey?'

The doctor grimaced slightly. 'It's a nasty burn but fortunately it's missed her eyes. She has actually mentioned her little girl, so perhaps you could tell her what's happened.'

Frankie moved to the side of the woman and smiled down at her. 'I thought you might like to know that Julie is in the children's ward at the moment—and she's fine. She's got a burn on her arm, but hopefully it will heal well and she won't even have a scar in a few months.'

Tracey tried to smile. 'Thank God for that,' she whispered. 'I thought everyone would die when the whole place went up.' Then she added more vehemently, 'I'll swing for that boyfriend of mine—I knew it was dodgy to tamper with the pipes. It was going to be such a happy afternoon, too.'

The woman's voice tailed off and she started to sob quietly, big tears rolling down her cheeks and over the dressing that had been applied to her face. Frankie stroked her hand gently.

'I'm sure they'll take you to see your little girl soon,' she said. 'Try not to worry.'

The situation seemed to be under control now, every patient having been stabilised and given emergency treatment. The usual reaction after coping with a serious incident hit Frankie—she felt absolutely drained and went to the staffroom to grab a hot drink. It had been a grim hour and she needed to get away for a little while. She went over to the window and looked out over the car park and the wooded area at the back of the hospital. It was a lovely sunny afternoon and everything looked so peaceful. Those people walking about outside could have no idea of the drama taking place in A and E or indeed in any of the hospital wards, she thought. Idly her eyes followed a man in the car park, trying to man- ouevre crutches out of a car and under his arms before setting off for the hospital entrance. There was something vaguely familiar about him. Then she yawned and started to turn away towards the cupboard where the mugs and coffee were kept. Two hands descended on her shoulders and made her jump.

'Had enough?' said Jack's familiar voice. 'Been quite an af- ternoon, hasn't it?' He pulled her round to him and looked down at her tired face. 'You look pretty knackered, sweetheart.'

Frankie smiled weakly at him. 'I feel pathetic really—if there's one scenario in A and E I find difficult, it's burns. I'm trying to control it, but it always gets to me…'

He smiled and hugged her to him for a second. 'No need to feel pathetic—everyone has their bugbears. I would never have known when you were dealing with that young man that it was giving you a hard time. You seemed very professional to me.'

She relaxed against him for a second, feeling great comfort in his words and physical presence. He brushed his lips across her forehead. 'I'm going to the children's ward to see Abby, but when she's dropped off to sleep why don't I take you home with me and I'll rustle up something pretty good to eat and a bottle of something to go with it? Then afterwards…'

She looked up at him mischievously. 'Afterwards? Well, it'll be time for bed, won't it?'

'Just what I thought.' He grinned. 'And that would be just what the doctor ordered!'

It was amazing what a little TLC from a man you were in love with could do for a girl, reflected Frankie. Despite the gruelling afternoon she'd had, little thrills of happiness flickered through her—she couldn't help thinking of the future that beckoned between her and Jack.

'Dr Lovatt?' Cindy's face appeared round the door. 'Some guy to see you in Reception—says it's urgent.'

'Me?' said Frankie in surprise. 'Did he give his name—is he a patient?'

'No, he didn't give his name, but he looked as if he could do with medical attention!'

With that she withdrew and Frankie looked at Jack blankly. 'How odd. I don't know who'd come and see me here on a weekday afternoon. Ah, well, only one way to find out.'

She turned to leave and Jack caught her hand for a moment and pulled her back to him. 'See you later, honey,' he whispered, and kissed her lips and then her neck softly so that the blood began to pound in her veins.

She laughed softly. 'Someone's going to see us,' she said reprovingly.

He looked down into her eyes and smiled. 'I don't care. I don't care if the dean of the medical faculty sees us…'

Frankie almost skipped down the corridor. It was as if a switch had been flicked and the relationship between her and Jack had gone up several notches.

Jack watched her trim figure disappear down the corridor and smiled to himself as he poured out a strong cup of black coffee. He'd tried, heaven knew, he'd tried to distance himself from her, to ignore the overwhelming need he'd felt for Frankie ever since he'd found himself falling in love with her—his future sister-in-law—over a year ago at St Mary's. He'd even left the area, only to end up working with Frankie again a few months later.

It must have been fate that had brought them together again, and now she'd actually admitted that she loved him, surely he had no need to worry about whether it was on the rebound or that he'd be lumbering her with his problems. If Frankie loved him, she knew that meant taking on his daughter as well. For the first time in two years Jack began to feel an exhilarating happiness he'd thought he'd never feel again. He tossed back the rest of his coffee and grinned idiotically at himself in the mirror above the basin, then went to phone a consultant on the burns unit about one of the patients they'd been treating.

Frankie decided she would pop in to see Abby later and go to the hospital shop as soon as her shift ended to buy a toy for the little girl. The automatic doors into Reception slid open as she went through and she stood by the desk and scanned the area where patients and their relatives were waiting to be seen.

A man was standing by the exit—a tall blond man wearing a tracksuit and with crutches under his arms. At first Frankie didn't recognise him, then he turned towards her and their eyes met. A livid red scar ran down the side of his face, and he was on crutches. One of the legs of the tracksuit was doubled up underneath the knee, and it was obvious that he had lost one leg. It took a few seconds for Frankie to realise that it was Damian.

CHAPTER TEN

TIME SEEMED TO stand still for a moment. People bustled by, a child cried and in the corner a television was showing a football match, but Frankie heard nothing of that. All she was aware of was Damian standing across the room from her, those pale blue eyes and lopsided grin directed towards her.

'My God,' she whispered, almost staggering backwards with the shock. 'What…what on earth are you doing here?'

He started to make his way towards her, rather awkwardly but by no means slowly. Then he propped his crutches on a chair and took her arms, looking deeply into her eyes. 'Frankie, darling…how are you?'

Frankie's voice was choked, forcing its way out of her throat. 'Damian…what's happened to you? How did you get this scar? And your leg—was it a road accident?'

He laughed, that familiar infectious laugh. 'Can't say it was an accident, sweetheart. I told you the island was a danger-ous spot and I got in the line of fire a few weeks ago.'

Suddenly Frankie felt very weak, as if someone had just hit her very hard in the solar plexus. She put out a hand to steady herself on the desktop. 'I can't believe you're here.' She touched the scar on his face gently. 'And this was part of the line of fire? And your leg?'

''Fraid so. I won't be taking part in any marathons for the time being…but give me a few months and I'll be running again.'

Frankie's eyes filled with tears. Whatever had happened between her and Damian, he had always been physically brave, brushing aside danger to himself.

'I'm so sorry Damian…' she whispered.

'Ah, well, life goes on…' He shrugged as if his injuries were no more than a temporary nuisance. Then he put his hands on her shoulders and looked down at her teasingly. 'Well, after all this time, haven't you got a kiss for your ex-fiancé?'

One hand went behind her head, pulling her towards him, and before she could protest, he had kissed her hard on her lips. 'Can't tell you how much I've been looking forward to that,' he said when he released her.

She wrenched herself away from him and looked at him with astonishment, completely taken unawares, then said in a cold, low voice, 'What the hell do you think you're doing? I'm not your fiancée any more. I seem to remember you writing me a letter, finishing our relationship. You didn't even have the guts to tell me you'd become engaged to Betsy St John, and I can assure you that any relationship we had together is over.'

He raised one eyebrow. 'Come on, that was just a silly publicity stunt. These film stars like a good story. I thought it would be a laugh.'

Frankie was suddenly aware that people sitting in chairs near them were looking at her and Damian with interest. If she wasn't careful, the whole hospital would know of the scenario.

'Follow me,' she said brusquely. 'We can't talk here.'

She led him through to one of the empty cubicles then put her hands on her hips and said icily, 'So that's the story, is it? Just publicity for a tacky film star?'

He laughed. 'That's my old feisty Frankie. I tell you, it was just a joke, a stupid piece of journalese that I never dreamed would get in the national papers.'

'Evidently.'

He put his hand on her arm, his lips quirked in a little smile. 'You didn't believe that nonsense did you? It meant nothing, as I've said. It was just a bit of fun. Please, Frankie, darling, where's your sense of humour?'

'My sense of humour?' Frankie stared at him furiously. How could she have fallen for such a clown? 'I'm sorry. You're free to marry anyone you want—what we had together is all water under the bridge now. But you might have told me the reason you wanted to break up with me.'

'She made a play for me, Frankie…'

'And you fell for it? More fool you. What's happened to her now?'

Damian's winning smile left his face for a moment. 'She wasn't very keen on marrying someone with a disability, I guess,' he muttered.

Frankie looked at his handsome face marred by a terrible scar and his athletic body changed for ever, and a pang of sympathy went through her. 'What exactly did happen to cause these injuries?' she asked in a softer voice.

'One of the people at the factory had apparently been hiding drugs there and hadn't paid for them. A few of his friends turned up for the money, and they didn't care who got hurt in the process…'

'And you were in the way?'

He nodded, and for the first time a bitter expression crossed his face. 'A machete can do a lot of damage,' he commented.

Frankie's eyes widened in horror. 'Oh, God, how terrible. It's a miracle you weren't killed... And now you've come back—is that for good?'

'Oh, I couldn't live here—it's far too boring,' he said carelessly.

'Then why have you come?'

'I came back because I was desperate to see you—and while I'm here I'll have to drum up some more money for the factory. It's beginning to take off now!' The charming smile lit his face again. 'And how are your parents? I'm sure your father would be interested in a good investment, wouldn't he?'

It was so blatant, so calculated, thought Frankie. The film star had given him the push, so it was back to square one and Frankie Lovatt with her wealthy, generous parents. She looked at him full in the face, her brown eyes sharp and her face as hard as granite.

'I'm sorry, Damian—sorry about what's happened to you—but I don't want to see you or hear from you again,' she said coldly. 'I'll have to go now. I'm still on duty and we're very busy...and I have nothing more to say to you.'

'You can't mean that, babe.' He caught her arm as she passed him. 'You can't just leave me like that—after all, we were together for a long time. I must see you after work. I need to discuss things. And, remember, you did say once you'd wait for me for ever.'

And people changed their minds, thought Frankie, pausing by the door and looking back at him. Now she'd fallen for another man, someone who was reliable and trustworthy, who didn't want to hog the limelight. Someone who wouldn't discard her like an old glove when a more exciting offer came along.

She pulled herself up to her full height and folded her arms in front of her. 'Damian, I'm afraid there won't be any going back to how things were. The fact is I don't love you any more and I don't want to see you again. I've moved on now.'

A gleam of intelligence shone in Damian's pale eyes. 'Ah, you mean you've met someone else?' He laughed scornfully. 'It won't last. I'm back now, and we're going to be together.'

'Don't be ridiculous,' grated Frankie as she went out of the room and walked quickly down to the main desk. Behind her Damian stood in the doorway and called after her.

'See you after work. I'll be waiting.'

She made no reply but quickened her pace away from him.

Jack pushed his way through the queue in the cafeteria and pushed a paper cup into the coffee-machine, punching the button to activate it. Then he slumped gloomily into a chair and absently stirred sugar into the black liquid. What the hell was Damian doing back in the country and why had he come to see Frankie? No prizes for guessing, Jack thought cynically. It was obvious that something terrible had happened in South America to cause Damian's injuries, and now he'd come running for home and the beautiful, faithful Francesca, whom he hadn't hesitated to dump when it had suited him.

Jack had seen it all from the door of the reception area where he'd gone to meet the consultant he'd been phoning on the burns unit. He'd seen the passionate kiss between Damian and Frankie, her hand going up to caress Damian's face and her expression when she'd first seen him—horror then compassion. There was a hollow feeling in the pit of Jack's stomach as he tried to come to terms with the fact that it was clear Frankie still felt something for the man. She would want to look after Damian now he was disabled, and all the angst he had caused her would be forgotten.

Damian always got what he wanted in the end, reflected Jack bitterly.

He clenched his fists in his pockets—Frankie had told him she loved him, but that had been before she'd known that Damian had returned. And how did *he* feel about Damian— the man who'd once saved his life? Jack owed the man so much—they'd been best mates as well as brothers-in-law. Now, when Damian was disfigured and disabled, how could he, Jack, stand in the way of the man's happiness?

He pulled a piece of paper from his pocket and started to write furiously, then he leapt up from the table, startling a couple of nurses engaged in a conversation. Everything was clear—he'd have to remove himself from the scene. From now on, Frankie Lovatt was off limits, he thought savagely. There could be no future between them now Damian was back on the scene. He strode quickly from the room cafeteria and back to A and E, numbed by the bitter feeling of disappointment and unhappiness.

Corey was standing by the whiteboard, erasing some patients' names that had been dealt with and writing new ones in. She looked up at Jack as he came towards her.

'Oh, Frankie wanted to tell you something—she says it's important.'

'Tell her I know what it is already,' said Jack grimly. 'Give this to her, will you? My shift's over and I'm going to go and see Abby in the children's ward now.' He handed her the note.

'Do you want me to ask her—'

Corey gazed after him, puzzled, as he strode off as if the cavalry were after him without replying. She shrugged and continued with her job. He'd looked rather upset—perhaps he and Frankie had had a tiff. She smiled to herself. It was so obvious to her that those two had the hots for each other, although neither of them had said anything. And how well suited they were, Corey thought. After all Frankie's upset over her broken engagement, Jack would be just the cure for a broken heart.

There was a rapping noise on the desk behind her. Corey turned round and was confronted by a large man in a dinner suit.

'I need to see a doctor. I've been sent through here from Reception but the place seems deserted.' His voice was abrupt, the kind of tone that brooked no argument.

'Perhaps you'd come through to this cubicle,' said Corey, wondering why the most demanding patients always turned up just at the end of a shift. 'I'll just take your details.'

The man sighed impatiently. 'For goodness' sake, I gave the receptionist all the information you require—all this red tape and duplication…'

Corey flicked a glance down the corridor. Frankie was walking towards her. 'Dr Lovatt, I wonder if you'd take a look at the patient in this cubicle—he's been sent through from Reception?'

'Of course,' said Frankie brightly. Her mind was working on autopilot, every emotion in the book whirling around in her head. She still could hardly believe that she'd just seen

Damian, or that he'd had the unmitigated cheek to think that
her parents would be pleased to give him more money for his
damn factory, and that she and he would get back together.

'At last!' said the man as Frankie entered the cubicle.

'Good afternoon,' she said politely. 'How can we help?'

'I've been waiting here for three hours…I repeat, three
hours,' said the man loudly, tapping the top of a cupboard top
as he spoke. 'It's absolutely disgraceful. I thought there were
time limits in Casualty.'

Frankie sighed, experienced enough to know that this was
the sort of man who was hard to placate. She felt dangerously
near the end of her tether—all the happy excitement she'd felt
with Jack was mixed up with the extraordinary and unexpected appearance of Damian.

'Well, what's your problem, Mr…?'

'Grenville-Watts—Richard Grenville-Watts.' He stuck a
large plump hand under Frankie's nose. 'That's my problem,
Doctor—a very irritating rash. I think I must be allergic to
something.'

Frankie peered at it. There was a faint raised red mark
over the palm of his hand. 'How long have you had it?'

'A few days—it's been driving me mad.'

'I see. Did you not think of going to your GP?'

He gave a sarcastic grunt. 'Impossible to get an appointment in the evening, and I'm far too busy in the morning with
meetings. Now I've got to go to a dinner…' He shot a look at
an expensive gold watch. 'I'm going to be late if you don't
get a move on.'

Frankie folded her arms and tapped her foot. She reflected
that any minute she might explode if she had any more aggro

that afternoon. 'My job, Mr Grenville-Watts,' she said with a slight inflection on the word 'job', 'is to deal with seriously injured people, or those patients who have life-threatening medical conditions. This afternoon we have had a great number of them and that is the reason you've had to wait, I dare say.'

Richard Grenville-Watts looked slightly abashed. 'I'm not saying my complaint is life-threatening—I'm saying it needs looking at before it gets worse…'

He drew breath to make some more observations and just then there was the high-pitched squeal of the emergency cardiac signal that alerted any medical staff within reach to get to the scene of a cardiac arrest. Frankie ran out of the cubicle saying over her shoulder, 'Sorry Mr Grenville-Watts, we have an emergency—a real emergency. You may be forced to wait some more…'

The man looked at his watch in disgust and stalked out of the department, muttering only to the receptionist as he passed her, 'Call this an accident and emergency unit?'

The team tried to save the old lady who'd been brought in with a heart attack, but it was, as Sister Kenney said, a lost cause. The patient was very old and had reached the end of her life and had been suffering from progressive heart failure for a long time.

The woman's daughter wiped her eyes and said tearfully, 'I wouldn't have wanted Mum to go on as she was…but thank you all of you for trying so hard. I do appreciate your kindness.'

Corey had brought her a cup of tea and she sat in the room reserved for relatives while Frankie spent some time with her as they discussed Mrs Monkton's long and happy life. When the daughter had left, Frankie turned to Corey and sighed.

'What a day! I feel as if I've been run over by a steamroller.'

'No worse than many,' remarked Corey, as she tidied the magazines on the table in the relatives' room.

'For me it was,' said Frankie. 'If I told you Damian had turned up in Reception, would you believe me?'

Corey's mouth dropped open in amazement. '*What?* I don't believe it—are you sure?'

'Of course I'm sure, you idiot. He's been very badly injured. In fact, he's lost a leg in a horrible attack at his factory. And now he seems to think we should be back together.'

It was a lot of information for Corey to take in. She shook her head and sat down by Frankie on the sofa. 'He's lost a leg? That's terrible. How did it happen?' She looked at Frankie in puzzlement. 'And I thought he was engaged to that film star, Betsy someone or other?'

'He was,' said Frankie succinctly. 'She likes her men to be perfect physical specimens, however, so he's been abandoned. Apparently he was attacked by a gang looking for payment for drugs from some employee.'

'And now he's come back to you…'

'No way—I'll never go back to him,' declared Frankie vehemently.

'I should think not! You'd be a fool, Frankie, especially when…' Corey started to say something then bit her lip. It wasn't up to her to point out that Jack obviously loved Frankie—they had to sort things out themselves.

'That man's got a skin like a rhino,' continued Frankie. 'I've told him where to get off and I hope he's taken in on board—but I doubt it!'

'Well, I'm flabbergasted,' said Corey slowly. Then she

looked up at Frankie mischievously. 'You can always tell him that you've met someone else—which reminds me…' She put her hand in her pocket and took out the note Jack had given her. 'This is for you. Jack's finished now and gone to see his little girl—he asked me to give it you.'

'Thanks,' said Frankie. 'I'll wander over that way myself when I've finished—I'd like to see how Abby is and I've got a little book to give her from the shop.'

'A good idea,' said Corey with a grin. 'Perhaps Jack will still be with her. I'm sure he'd rather see you than correspond with you!'

Frankie made a face at her and went to check with Sister Kenney on the new admissions and to start the handover for the next shift. She felt exhausted after the emotional meeting with Damian and couldn't wait to see Jack and tell him what had happened. The next half-hour was very busy and it wasn't until she was collecting her bag and jacket from her locker that she remembered the note Corey had given her from Jack. She opened it up and read it quickly, then with a feeling of disbelief sat down slowly on the bench in front of her locker. The afternoon had produced far too many shocks.

'My darling Frankie,' she read. 'I'll be brief. Having just seen Damian and you together in Reception, I've put two and two together and realised that he has come back to reclaim you. I don't want to make things awkward for you. I see he must have had some terrible accident, and of course you will want to go back to him and look after him. I won't stand in your way, even though I love you totally. When I left St Mary's almost a year ago now without any warning, it was because I knew I was falling in love with you, and as brother-in-law to your fiancé, that was going to make life very difficult. I had to get away from you—try and make a new life for myself and Abby somewhere else. I even got engaged, trying to force myself to settle down with a nice girl who would be a good mother to Abby. That was grossly unfair to the girl and I soon realised that I should break it off and go and live nearer my parents and ask them to help with Abby.

'I won't leave the district this time, but I will try and move departments where perhaps we won't always be bumping into each other. You can pick up again where you left with Damian—I was always aware that you might still have some feelings for the man. From my point of view, I have to say I would not want to come between you two. I owe Damian a lot. He introduced me to his wonderful sister, Sue, and many years ago he saved my life at risk to his own. But most of all, my darling, I want your happiness above everything, and if that means I can't have you, so be it.

'Always know, however, I shall be around if you need me—friends for ever, I hope. My love, Jack.'

Frankie jumped to her feet, crumpling the note and stuffing it into her pocket. She was damned if she was going to allow Damian to take over her life again. Whatever Jack had seen between her and Damian, he'd got the wrong idea. Fury leant her wings and she almost galloped through the hospital to the children's ward where Corey had said Jack had gone to see Abby.

She stopped by the office at the entrance to the ward, where a nurse was writing up some notes.

'Is Jack Herrick in here, seeing his little girl?' she asked the nurse breathlessly.

The nurse looked up. 'You've just missed him,' she said. 'He's gone back home to see his parents.'

Frankie turned on her heel and ran back to the hospital exit that opened onto the car park. Perhaps she'd get him before he drove away. She stood for a moment at the entrance, shading her eyes from the late afternoon sun, straining to see if he was still there. Suddenly she saw his tall figure striding towards his car.

'Jack,' she screamed. 'Jack—I want to speak to you!'

He couldn't hear her, and in despair she set off at a run again, every breath hurting as she tried to get to him before he drove off. She pushed her way through several people meandering back to their vehicles, and eventually reached his car just as he had got in and slammed the door. She banged the boot with her hand and he turned round with a start. Then he saw who it was and slowly opened the door and got out. Frankie was gasping for breath and leaning against the car to recover.

'You read my note?' he said, watching her intently. She nodded, speechless for a second, and he continued, 'Then you'll know why I don't want to stand in your way. Damian needs you to look after him—and however much he hurt you with that silly business of the film star, I know you still love him really.'

She flushed hotly. 'You know nothing of the sort. What the hell makes you say that?'

'I saw you kiss—I saw the way you looked at him when you first realised he'd come back. You were full of compassion for him.'

'Of course I'm sorry for him—but that's as far as it goes.' Her voice trembled with suppressed anger. 'When I think how long I waited for him, trying to be loyal. Only when he needs something, such as money, does he bother to come back. No, Damian means nothing to me now. You know who I love.'

'He was my best friend, he saved me from drowning and his sister was my wife,' said Jack softly. 'I can't come between him and you.'

Frankie stamped her foot in frustration. 'For God's sake, I don't love the man—can't you understand? And I'm not a commodity to be weighed against how much you owe him.'

'She's right, you know!'

The voice came from a few feet away behind them. Frankie and Jack whirled round, suddenly back in the real world and aware that other people were near them. Damian was leaning against a car and regarding them both quizzically through the smoke of his cigarette.

'So,' he said laconically, flicking the stub away. 'It's as I thought. You have got someone else, sweetheart—although I have to admit, I never dreamt it would be Jack. How long has this been going on?'

'It's none of your business,' declared Frankie, 'but I can assure you it was after you got engaged to Betsy St John. I don't owe you any explanations, Damian.'

He laughed. 'I know, I know...' He turned to Jack and grinned his lopsided charming grin. 'All's fair in love and war and all I can say is, don't be a fool like me and let a gem like Frankie slip through your fingers.' An expression of sadness flitted across his face, so quickly that it was hard to tell it had been there. 'I guess I didn't deserve her—so, for Pete's sake, learn from my mistake and get married to the girl as quickly as you can!'

Then he picked up his crutches and gave them a half-wave, before turning and going back across the car park.

They looked after him silently for a minute, then Frankie said in a small voice, 'Poor Damian—I wonder if he'll ever find happiness?'

'He's a restless soul,' said Jack. 'I guess he needs excitement in his life—domesticity was never his thing.' Then he added slowly, 'You know, I think he was giving us his blessing.'

'Perhaps he was,' sighed Frankie. Then she said softly, 'Oh, Jack, why didn't you tell me ages ago you loved me?'

'For all the reasons I wrote down,' he said simply. 'When I first loved you, you weren't free, and when Damian and you split up you didn't want to start up a new relationship—you wanted to be your own person, you said, concentrate on your career. And, anyway, I thought I came with too much baggage from my past—a little girl to look after…'

'But I love Abby!' cried Frankie, 'And I know I said all those things, but after a very short time I knew I didn't mean them. I wanted you so badly, but then I thought…'

'You thought what?' asked Jack gently.

'I thought that you wouldn't or couldn't replace Sue…that you still loved her.'

Jack stepped forward and put his arms on her shoulders, looking down into her eyes with something so tender in his blue ones that her own filled with tears. 'My sweet, I loved Sue—of course I did, and I thought the world had ended when she died. But time heals and although I'll never forget her, it's you I love now. My time with Sue is a happy memory, but what I've wanted for so long is to look forward to a future with you…and Abby, of course…but I never thought it would be possible.'

His arms curved around her and he put his lips to hers and kissed her very gently, then he murmured, 'You once said you'd like Abby to be your bridesmaid. Perhaps she still can be, if I can be the groom?'

And Frankie looked up at him, a mischievous glint in her dark eyes and said, 'If that's a proposal, Jack Herrick, I accept!'

He folded her in his arms and kissed her passionately in response, and she hugged herself against him—and neither of them noticed that the weather had changed and that now it was pouring with rain.

From No. 1 *New York Times* bestselling author Nora Roberts

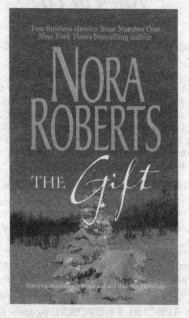

Two tales of love found at Christmas featuring

Home for Christmas

and

All I Want for Christmas

On sale 1st December 2006

MILLS & BOON®

Live the emotion

Medical romance™

THE SURGEON'S MEANT-TO-BE BRIDE
by Amy Andrews

Nurse Harriet Remy and her surgeon husband Guillaume thought they had the perfect marriage. Then Harriet's fertility came under threat and her subsequent desire for a baby came between them. After a year apart, Gill still adores his wife, and on a final overseas aid mission with her, decides this will also become a mission to save their marriage – and keep his wife by his side…for ever.

A FATHER BY CHRISTMAS *by Meredith Webber*

Neonatologist Sophie Fisher is bowled over by her new boss's strength and kindness. She hasn't yet told Gib that Thomas, the little boy in her care, is actually her nephew, and that she is trying to find his father. Gib is dedicated to his patients and not looking for love – though there is something about Sophie that is changing his mind. Then he makes a discovery about Thomas…

A MOTHER FOR HIS BABY *by Leah Martyn*

Dr Brady McNeal is hoping a new life for him and his tiny son will be just what they need, and the Mount Pryde Country Practice seems like a small slice of heaven – especially when he finds that he is working with GP Jo Rutherford. The attraction between Brady and Jo is undeniable. Soon Brady is wishing that Jo had a more permanent role in his life…

On sale 1st December 2006

Available at WHSmith, Tesco, ASDA, Borders, Eason, Sainsbury's and most bookshops

www.millsandboon.co.uk

FREE

4 BOOKS AND A SURPRISE GIFT!

We would like to take this opportunity to thank you for reading this Mills & Boon® book by offering you the chance to take FOUR more specially selected titles from the Medical Romance™ series absolutely FREE! We're also making this offer to introduce you to the benefits of the Mills & Boon® Reader Service™—

- ★ **FREE home delivery**
- ★ **FREE gifts and competitions**
- ★ **FREE monthly Newsletter**
- ★ **Books available before they're in the shops**
- ★ **Exclusive Reader Service offers**

Accepting these FREE books and gift places you under no obligation to buy; you may cancel at any time, even after receiving your free shipment. Simply complete your details below and return the entire page to the address below. You don't even need a stamp!

YES! Please send me 4 free Medical Romance books and a surprise gift. I understand that unless you hear from me, I will receive 6 superb new titles every month for just £2.80 each, postage and packing free. I am under no obligation to purchase any books and may cancel my subscription at any time. The free books and gift will be mine to keep in any case.

M6ZEE

Ms/Mrs/Miss/Mr..................................Initials ....
BLOCK CAPITALS PLEASE

Surname ....

Address ....

....

....Postcode ....

Send this whole page to:

The Reader Service, FREEPOST CN81, Croydon, CR9 3WZ